Truth Squad Trilogy:

Third Identity
Second Thoughts
First Priority

FIRST PRIORITY

KELSEY GJESDAL

WESTBOW
PRESS®
A DIVISION OF THOMAS NELSON
& ZONDERVAN

WestBow Press books may be ordered through booksellers or by contacting:

WestBow Press
A Division of Thomas Nelson & Zondervan
1663 Liberty Drive
Bloomington, IN 47403
www.westbowpress.com
844-714-3454

Scripture quotations are taken from the New American Standard Bible®, Copyright © 1960, 1962, 1963, 1968, 1971, 1972, 1973, 1975, 1977, 1995 by The Lockman Foundation. Used by permission.

ISBN: 978-1-6642-9046-4 (sc)
ISBN: 978-1-6642-9047-1 (hc)
ISBN: 978-1-6642-9045-7 (e)

Library of Congress Control Number: 2023901636

Print information available on the last page.

WestBow Press rev. date: 02/21/2023

CONTENTS

CHAPTER 1

"Hold it! Where do you think you're going?"

My heart skipped a beat as Daniel and I turned to face the security guard. "We were instructed to report to Mr. Greyson," I said, squaring my shoulders and raising an eyebrow. "I don't think it would be wise to keep him waiting."

The guard rolled his eyes. "I need to see your badges."

I grabbed my wallet from my back pocket and pulled out the fake badge with the name Jason Leanord I'd been using for the last three months. The guard grabbed my badge and looked it over, glancing at us with suspicion. After examining Daniel's badge, he shrugged and waved at the door. "Go ahead."

Daniel grabbed the handle and pulled the door open, and we hurried inside. "That guard is getting annoying," he muttered as we sped down the hall.

I shrugged. "Let's just hope we can get some good evidence today. I'm not sure how much longer this operation will last before we're caught."

Daniel nodded. We stopped talking as we reached the door for the manager's office. I knocked lightly on the door. I heard a grunt from inside, and then heavy footsteps coming toward the door. The door opened and Mr. Greyson waved us inside. "Come in," he said, his voice gruff.

We walked past the giant, red-bearded man and stood in front of his desk. He slowly closed the door and lumbered over to his desk, plopping down into his large, leather chair.

"You called for us?" I asked, raising my eyebrows.

Mr. Greyson nodded his balding head. "Have a seat. I have an assignment for you two."

I glanced at Daniel as we sat down. *Maybe we will get the evidence we need,* I thought hopefully.

"I've seen your hard work and determination, and I believe you are the right fit for the job." He paused and leaned forward, resting his crossed arms on the edge of the desk. "But first, tell me what you know about our parent company."

"You were formerly affiliated with the Patrick Brian Power Company and are now under the East-West Nuclear Company," Daniel said.

I nodded. "And that company is headed by MAX."

Mr. Greyson was silent for a moment, his eyes wide. *Oh, no. Should I not have mentioned MAX? Did I just blow our cover?* I thought.

After an agonizing ten seconds, Mr. Greyson smiled. "Yes, I believe you two are right for the job."

Thank You, Lord! I prayed as I slowly released the breath I was holding. "What would you like us to do, sir?"

"I'm in need of some, shall we say, cover for some recent mishaps," he said slowly, obviously choosing his words carefully.

"Mishaps?" Daniel asked.

Mr. Greyson nodded. "We have some financial issues to smooth out and some fired employees to keep quiet. I've already got someone on the financial side of things, so I need you to keep these former employees quiet."

"How do you propose doing so?" Daniel asked, glancing at me out of the corner of his eye.

He shrugged. "Money is usually a fine starting point."

"And suppose they won't take money to be quiet, or keep asking for more?" I raised my eyebrows. "How would you like it handled?"

"I'd hate to do anything drastic, but if it must be done, it must be done."

Daniel and I made eye contact, and I knew we were thinking the same thing. Daniel pushed the record button on his watch, and I quickly said, "Do you mean..."

"I mean whatever is necessary to keep them quiet," Mr. Greyson interrupted.

That's not a confession, I thought, trying to think up a question that we could get evidence from. "Has this ever happened before?" I asked.

Mr. Greyson's face grew stern. "You seem hesitant, Mr. Leanord. Are you telling me you don't want this job?"

I shook my head, trying to think fast. "It's not that. I just don't want to do anything too, you know, risky."

Mr. Greyson's face softened, and he rested his elbows on the desk, leaning toward us. "Look, I don't really like to order anything extreme. MAX prefers we 'eliminate' anyone who could be a potential threat, but I don't feel that way. That's why we always start with money. Most people are satisfied with a little extra cash, and we don't have to do any dirty work."

I nodded slowly. "So, have you ever had to do any 'dirty work?'"

He looked away and sighed. "I wish I could say no, but, well, MAX...." He sighed and ran a hand over his beard. "MAX is particular. If MAX finds out that I've been paying people off instead of 'eliminating' them, I could get in deep trouble."

"So, if MAX finds out about someone, they're eliminated?" Daniel asked.

Mr. Greyson nodded. "Precisely."

I glanced at Daniel. He nodded his head slightly and tapped his watch. The man had just confessed, and we recorded it.

"I need you two to keep on the low about this conversation, and get to work on bribing," Mr. Greyson said, standing. "Can I count on you?"

We stood and shook his hand. "Yes, sir."

After being handed a list of names, Daniel and I hurried out of Mr. Greyson's office and out of the building. Once we were safely in our car and driving away, I let my celebration loose. "Yes!" I said, doing a fist-pump. "We have our evidence! Have you sent the recording to Truth Squad?"

"I'm doing that right now," Daniel replied. "But why don't you keep both hands on the wheel, Luke?"

"Oops, sorry about that," I said, placing my hands in their proper ten-and-two spots. I didn't feel like driving with one hand was a bad idea, especially since most vehicles had at least partial, if not full, autopilot, but Daniel preferred to be a little less risky than me.

A couple minutes later, Daniel's smartphone rang. He put it on speaker, and Mr. Truth's voice rang out. "Great work, Luke and Daniel. This recording is exactly the information we needed. We got the information to the FBI, and we will be meeting with them to plan our next move as soon as you get back to base."

"Yes, sir," Daniel said.

"Great work, agents. See you in an hour." Mr. Truth ended the call.

"Bummer. He didn't even give us time to stop for a doughnut or ice-cream celebration or anything," I said, my shoulders drooping.

"We could save that celebration till after we've finished the mission entirely," Daniel said, running his hand over his light brown hair.

"Hey, every small step is worth celebrating," I replied, grinning.

"If I celebrated every small step with doughnuts, I don't think I could stay fit for my job," Daniel replied, patting his stomach.

"If we threw vegetables on top of our doughnuts, we'd be good to go."

Daniel laughed. "I don't think Rebecca would fall for that one, but it'd be worth a shot."

After our short flight from Colorado to Truth Squad's base in Oregon, Daniel and I hurried to the conference room to meet with Mr. Truth and the FBI. As we sped-walked through campus, I breathed in the damp fall air with a smile, having missed this beautiful campus I called home. Daniel and I had spent the majority of the past three months in Colorado as we worked undercover at Mr. Greyson's power plant. Our flights back to base were always short and work-related. More than missing Truth Squad's campus, I missed a special someone. Rebecca.

Inside the conference room we found Mr. Truth, the president of Truth Squad, my good friend Matthew, who was the vice-president of Truth Squad, and our FBI contact, Agent Brandon, along with Agent Holton, a younger agent who'd been working with us and Brandon on the MAX case.

"Good evening, gentlemen," I said as I took my seat at the large table.

Mr. Truth nodded. "Glad to have you two back. We're waiting for the rest of Squad 4 to arrive, and then we'll begin our meeting."

I smiled, excited to plan the next steps in our mission, but also excited to see all of my colleagues and friends. Truth Squad was an amazing organization to work for. I'd practically grown up at Truth Squad, having attended Truth Academy for all of my schooling and living on campus since my high-school years. Truth Squad was a private organization whose mission was to defend the truth in the United States and around the world, especially the truth of the gospel. We often partnered with the FBI and CIA, taking on important cases nationally and internationally that weren't the government's top priority. This situation, however, was different. For the past year and a half, we had been working with the FBI to track down a mysterious operation headed by the code name MAX.

The conference door swung open, shaking me from my thoughts. I smiled as the Squad 4 agents filed into the room, taking their usual places around the table. I high-fived my fellow special operations agents as they joined our section of the table. We all sat with our specialty group, mine being special-ops and undercover work.

My heart jumped as I saw the last two people enter the room – Sarah and Rebecca. *Why is Rebecca joining us?* I wondered, trying to hold back my excitement at seeing her.

Rebecca wasn't a Squad 4 member, although she had the skills to be one. Four years ago, she wasn't even at Truth Squad. She had worked for a former assassin and MAX leader named Richard Zaiden. He had been training her to be a top agent in their operation. Her identical twin sister, Sarah, and I had been assigned to go uncover a scam at a local power company in Seattle, which is where we ran into Rebecca and learned about Mr. Zaiden. Rebecca hadn't initially wanted to help us take out his operation, but eventually she had a change of heart, became a Christian, and helped us stop Mr. Zaiden's work. Due to her help, she was allowed to come to Truth Squad on parole, to test out a program Mr. Truth was interested in, instead of spending years in prison. Until she completed her parole, she was not allowed to become an official Truth Squad member. However, due to her connection with MAX, she had been called upon many times to help us with different missions as we tried to locate this MAX operation.

Rebecca leaned against the wall opposite from me and smiled. I smiled back, then turned my attention to Mr. Truth as he filled the group in on the details Daniel and I had uncovered.

"We believe that we now have the evidence necessary to put a stop to this operation, and we are requesting Truth Squad's participation in doing so," Agent Brandon explained.

"Agent Brandon and I have already begun planning our operation to close the plant and hopefully get more information on MAX. Let me pull up the plans," Mr. Truth said, tapping on the large screen on the wall.

I smiled, excitement pumping through my veins. *Let's do this.*

"You ready?" Daniel asked as we walked up to the front doors of the power plant.

"Oh yeah." I grinned and pulled the door open.

We hurried to our office cubicles and began our usual work, waiting for the signal in our coms from the FBI. Agent

Brandon and Mr. Truth had decided that Daniel and I needed to continue working as usual at the plant so that if we needed to go undercover at another MAX operation, we wouldn't be recognized as undercover agents.

Time ticked by slowly as I filled out paperwork, waiting for the signal that Truth Squad was going into action.

The intercom clicked on, and Mr. Greyson's voice boomed, "Jason Leanord and Tim Jonson to my office please."

Hearing our aliases, Daniel and I both got up and hurried to the elevator. "I wonder what this meeting's about," Daniel muttered as we stepped into the elevator.

"Hopefully this doesn't mess up Mr. Truth's plans. We were supposed to be in our cubicles the whole time," I whispered.

The doors opened and we hurried down the hall, showed our badges to the security guard, and made our way to Mr. Greyson's office.

Mr. Greyson met us with a grim look on his face. "I have a change of plans for your work today," he said as we took our seats.

"What's the problem?" I asked. *Has he gotten wind of Truth Squad's plans?*

"I received word from my boss that we need to pack up some of our files and move them to another location," he said shaking his head. "Sounds like we may have an unexpected investigation today, and we don't want any loose ends to be found."

So, his boss may know about our operation? I wondered, glancing at Daniel. He raised his eyebrows, and I figured he was thinking the same thing.

"I've already got some other employees working on this, but we need to move faster. I need you two down this hall in the second room on the right packing up boxes. Work as fast as you can and make sure everything is out of that room in the next hour. There are boxes in the hallway you can use. I will pay you extra for this," Mr. Greyson said. He pulled a key out of a drawer and slid it across his desk.

"You got it," I said, grabbing the key. The fact that he was bribing us made me nervous. *What exactly are we packing up?* I wondered as we left his office and went to the designated room. I unlocked the door and pushed it open. The room was lined with file cabinets, and there were stacks of paper scattered on the floor. In the center of the room was a rectangular metal box with a computer on the left side, a bunch of switches numbered one through seventy in the middle, and a big lever on the right. There were blinking lights all over the face of the box.

"What is this?" Daniel asked, walking up to the box.

"I have no clue," I said, walking around it. "It looks like it's bolted to the floor, though, so I'm not sure we'll be moving it from the room." On the back side of the table, I found a little door. I tried to open it, but it was locked.

"Maybe there are keys in some of these file cabinets," Daniel suggested. "Either way, we'd better start packing up the cabinets before Mr. Greyson gets suspicious."

I nodded. "Let's hope Mr. Truth starts the operation before all the evidence is moved out of the building."

We worked quickly, transferring stack after stack of paper from the floor and the cabinets to the cardboard boxes Mr. Greyson left outside the door. The papers seemed to call my name, telling me to look through them and find out why Mr. Greyson wanted them packed up so quickly, but I restrained myself. *Once Truth Squad gets in here, we'll be able to look through these papers. For now, just don't act suspicious and keep doing what you're told,* I told myself.

At the end of the hour, we had all the papers in boxes and began carrying them out to a moving truck. *Why hasn't Truth Squad made their move yet?* I wondered as I set another box onto the truck.

Daniel and I exchanged glances as we walked back inside. Once we were in the elevator, I whispered, "What time did Mr. Truth say they were going to come?"

"Over an hour ago." He shook his head. "Something doesn't seem right. They haven't even signaled us to let us know that plans changed."

I glanced down at my watch. "Actually, I've noticed ever since we entered this half of the building that my watch isn't working. There's no signal."

The elevator doors opened, and we quit talking. We grabbed a new load of boxes and headed back to the elevator. Daniel nudged me and nodded toward the corner above the elevator. I looked up and saw a black box, one that looked similar to other transmission blockers I'd worked with.

We stepped into the elevator and put our boxes down. I hit the first-floor button and the doors closed. The elevator started descending, when suddenly there was a loud bang. The elevator shook and the lights flickered off.

I grinned at Daniel. "I believe the cavalry has arrived."

"No kidding!" He glanced around the elevator. "But I didn't expect the power to go out. Should we try to get out of the elevator or stay in till they come find us?"

I looked at my watch, noticing there was still no signal. "I think we should leave the elevator. We can't contact them from in here, and I think to look convincing to Mr. Greyson we should try to escape."

Daniel nodded. "Let's try the safety hatch, then," he said, pointing to the ceiling.

I climbed up on my box and turned the red handle to the hatch door. After some effort it turned, and I pushed the hatch open. I glanced back at Daniel. "Should we try to take the boxes with us, or leave them here?"

"Leave them."

I nodded and grabbed onto the edges of the elevator hatch. I jumped and pulled myself up through the hole onto the top of the elevator. Daniel climbed up and then we looked around for the nearest exit. There were elevator doors about ten feet above us, and a metal ladder ran up the side of the wall left of the doors.

"How do we get the door open when we get up there?" Daniel asked, raising an eyebrow.

I shrugged. "Do you think there's an emergency opening or something?"

"If there is, it probably requires power," Daniel said. He crossed his arms. "Too bad there's not a ladder on each side, then we could each pull the door open from opposite sides."

"We'll just have to try and pull it open on one side. Let's go."

I grabbed hold of the ladder and started climbing, Daniel following close behind. Once I was level with the door, I looked around it for some way to force the door open. I sighed. "No open door buttons or any tools to pry the door open. Looks like we'll just have to use our muscles."

Daniel flexed his bicep. "Good thing I work out."

Holding onto the ladder with my left hand, I reached out my right hand and forced my fingers between the closed doors. I pulled at the door. It didn't budge.

"Climb up a little higher so I can reach the door and we can pull together," Daniel suggested.

I nodded and pulled my fingers out from between the doors. After climbing a few more rungs, I reached back over to the door. "Ready, Daniel?"

"On three," he replied. "One, two, three!" We pulled with all our might. The door groaned and slowly began to open. Once there was enough space, Daniel slid through the door, and I swung inside behind him.

"Whew!" I sighed, wiping sweat from my forehead.

"We'd better start our getaway," Daniel said.

We hurried toward the nearest stairwell. I glanced around, noticing how empty this floor was. *Did Mr. Greyson have everyone move out of here, too? How did his boss know what was happening today?* I wondered.

We hurried down the stairs and out the back door, running toward the edge of the property. As we neared the chain-link fence, we heard Matthew's familiar voice yell, "Stop right where you are! Do not take another step or I'll shoot. Turn around slowly with your hands in the air."

Daniel and I grinned at each other before turning around and raising our hands, quickly changing our expressions. Until the operation was completed, Daniel and I had to act the part of Mr. Greyson's employees.

After handcuffing us, Matthew escorted us to the front of the building where the other employees were, guarded by Sarah, Rebecca, and a few FBI agents.

"Got a couple more for you," Matthew called.

Rebecca smirked. "Wonderful. Have a seat, gentlemen."

I suppressed a smile and replied, "Whatever you say, milady."

Once the FBI had all the right people in custody and the property cleared, Daniel and I were brought back to survey the information we'd gained.

"Did you catch the moving truck with all the papers?" I asked as we walked inside.

"We found the truck down the road a little ways," Matthew said, "But someone had set fire to the papers, so a lot of them aren't salvageable."

I shook my head. "That stinks."

"But there is one thing we want to show you," Matthew said. He led us up the stairs back to the floor of Mr. Greyson's office.

My eyes widened as I saw the smoke-stained hallway. "Someone set fire to the things left up here, too."

Matthew nodded. "We got the fire out pretty quickly, so we saved more of the papers from here than from the truck." He opened the door to the room with the file cabinets. "I want to know what that monstrosity was." He pointed to the charred remains of the large black box in the center of the room.

I shrugged. "I don't know. It had levers and lights on it, and a computer, but today was the first time I saw it."

Daniel nodded. "I've never seen anything like it before."

Matthew walked around the box, pulling on the edges. "It feels solid still. Maybe we can open it up and find some clues on the inside."

"So, did Truth Squad cause the power outage, or was it Mr. Greyson?" I asked, raising an eyebrow.

"It wasn't us. It must have been a diversion. It gave him enough time to set fire to all the things he didn't want us to see," Matthew said, shrugging.

"Did you apprehend him?" Daniel asked.

Matthew nodded. "He's being interrogated by the FBI right now." We walked back out of the room and down the stairs. "What else did you learn?"

"Well, when Mr. Greyson called us to his office today, he said his boss got word of an unexpected investigation," I said, opening the door to the first floor.

Daniel nodded. "He had us load up everything from that room onto the moving truck. We were hoping you guys would get here sooner so we could see why he was in a hurry to pack up those papers."

I nodded. "What took you so long, anyway? Stopped for a doughnut run or something?"

Matthew rolled his eyes at my joke. "No, the FBI surprised us with extra red tape to get through. We tried to contact you about the delay but none of our messages got through."

"Yeah, they had transmission blockers up in the back half of the building," I explained as we walked out the front door.

"Hey," Daniel said, nodding his head toward the side of the building. Matthew and I followed him around the corner. Daniel glanced around before whispering, "Matthew, you said the FBI held you up before you could get here?"

Matthew nodded. "Why do you ask?"

"I'm just wondering if MAX had someone on the inside informing him of the FBI's arrival."

"You think they have a mole in the FBI?" I said, crossing my arms. "I guess it would make sense. A lot of the MAX operations we've infiltrated have gotten rid of evidence right before we showed up to shut them down."

Matthew cocked his head thoughtfully. "MAX seems to have roots all over the US, so it's highly probable that they've got contacts in the FBI. The fact that they've outmaneuvered every one of our operations with the FBI is suspicious."

"They're very smart about it though," I said, tapping my chin. "I mean, they've never kept us from shutting down any plants, they just get rid of any evidence we need to find MAX."

"So, obviously these small operations don't matter too much to MAX, and they want us and the FBI to think we're onto something when we're not," Daniel suggested. He sighed. "I think we need to be on the lookout for a MAX agent in the FBI."

"Agreed," Matthew said, nodding.

And we need to think of a better way to outsmart MAX, I thought. But how?

Late that evening we were back at Truth Squad, seated around the conference table debriefing about our mission. Mr. Truth stood at the head of the table, listening to the reports we'd brought back. He looked the part of the president of Truth Squad with his broad shoulders, angular jaw, dark hair sprinkled with gray, and bright blue eyes that became laser-focused during missions. Matthew stood by the wall-mounted computer, recording notes on the mission. He was six foot three, and as teenagers he enjoyed rubbing in the fact that he was two inches taller than me, but I would remind him that he was also three years older. He was also insanely muscular and was one of the best agents at Truth Squad. He had brown hair and hazel eyes and was no-nonsense when it came to Truth Squad missions.

"So, it appears that the little info we were able to gather shows that we have again confirmed that MAX is targeting power plants," Matthew said, pointing to the bullet-points on the screen. "Mr. Greyson's company was apparently not very high up in MAX's operation, because he has never met the leader of MAX, he didn't know much about what was going on, and he had only become aware of the operation after Mr. Zaiden's power plant was closed four years ago."

Daniel raised a hand as he straightened his broad shoulders. "Matthew, may I speak to the theory on the FBI?"

Matthew nodded. "I was just about to ask you to do so."

Daniel quickly launched into a recap of his thoughts on a MAX agent infiltrating the FBI. "At the very least, they must have hacked the system somewhere, if not placed MAX agents into the FBI."

Mr. Truth nodded thoughtfully. "That could very well be a possibility. Rebecca, what's your thoughts on this theory?"

I glanced across the table at Sarah and Rebecca. The twenty-two-year-old identical twins sat side-by-side, both sitting completely straight with their long, wavy brown hair pulled back in a braid. Both of them had blue eyes and pale skin, and were close to the same height. Today Rebecca wore a blue Truth Squad t-shirt, while Sarah wore her Truth Squad uniform, making them easier to tell apart.

Rebecca cleared her throat. "I think Daniel's theory is on-point. We've seen that MAX's operation is nationwide, and if the boss is anything like Zaiden, he would definitely place agents inside the FBI to keep his operation in hiding."

"Matthew, refresh us on what we know about MAX so far," Mr. Truth said, waving at the screen.

Matthew pulled up a folder labeled "MAX" and opened it, revealing a document of notes on the operation. "MAX has taken over power plants all over the US and seems especially interested in nuclear energy. From Mr. Zaiden's case we learned they are interested in US security documents and EMPs. We know they have been collecting stolen firearms, and he hires hitmen to take out defecting agents. We know MAX needed some codes from Mr. Zaiden and tried to get them from Rebecca a couple years ago, and since that time one other hitman has been sent to Truth Squad to try and get rid of her but failed. Most operations we have shut down have been connected to agents who were connected to MAX and didn't have a direct line of communication with the head man. We also have reason to believe that the MAX headquarters may be closer to the East Coast since all of the operations we've shut down on the West Coast, aside from Mr. Zaiden's, have been small power companies and the directors have not personally communicated with MAX headquarters." Matthew took a deep breath.

"Don't forget, MAX activity seems to have boosted this year," Sarah added, raising her hand. "And some of the papers we recovered today seemed to indicate a connection between a big plan and November."

"Which happens to be election season," I said, raising my eyebrows.

Mr. Truth nodded. "That may be a coincidence, or it may be intentional. The problem is, we don't know anything about this big plan."

"It's already September," Daniel said, shaking his head. "We need some leads soon, otherwise we will just be responding to this big plan instead of preventing it."

Mr. Truth nodded. "If that's all the information we have so far, then why don't we spend some time in prayer? We may not have the answers, but God does. Let's surrender this to Him and trust that He will reveal the truth and bring about justice in His own good way." He glanced at me and raised his eyebrows. "Luke, will you pray?"

I smiled. "It would be my pleasure, sir."

I stretched as I walked out of the conference building, glancing down at my uniform. It was a bright blue long-sleeved button up shirt with matching blue pants, tall black boots, and a black belt. On the left sleeve was an American Flag patch, and on the right sleeve was the Truth Squad insignia. The back of our shirts read Truth Squad, and on the front we each had a patch with our rank and specialty denoted by different colors.

I smiled at Rebecca as she walked out of the building. "What'd you think about today's mission?"

She smiled. "It was great! Although I'm sure your undercover work was much more exciting."

I grinned. "It was pretty awesome, if I do say so myself." I yawned. "But it has been a long day. Do you want some doughnuts?"

"Did you say doughnuts?" Daniel called from behind. He came up and grasped my shoulder. "How did I know you were going to suggest that?"

"I have no clue," I said, faking innocence as I widened my brown eyes and ran my fingers through my dark brown hair.

"Not that you were talking to me, but I'd like a doughnut," he said, winking. "And I'm sure Sarah and Rebecca would love to join us."

"If we must," Rebecca said, her voice sarcastic but a sly grin on her face.

Sarah rolled her eyes at her sister. "I'd love a doughnut." Despite being the most identical looking twins I'd ever met, their personalities were opposites. Rebecca was sarcastic, craved excitement and loved dangerous missions, and hid her emotions. Sarah was very sweet, preferred safer missions, and didn't hide her emotions.

"Then let's go!" I said, heading toward the mess hall.

I loved my doughnuts. Many agents commented on my skinny frame and the number of doughnuts I ate a week, telling me that someday my metabolism would slow down and I couldn't eat so much junk food. It didn't seem like that time had come yet, though, so I figured I might as well keep enjoying my doughnuts.

Most people were surprised to find out I was a Squad Four agent. Even though I was twenty-two, I still looked like a teenager, unlike Daniel, who'd looked like he was in his twenties since he was sixteen and had had broad shoulders forever. My shoulders were just now starting to fill out, and despite working out along with all my co-agents, I still looked skinny. Despite my doughnut eating habits, I maintained a healthy diet to fuel my non-stop energy and creativity. Not only was I an undercover agent, but I also loved tinkering with gadgets and creating new inventions.

We each got a doughnut from the kitchen, then went back outside and sat at one of the picnic tables. It was a cool fall night without any rain, a perfect evening.

"You two glad to be done with your mission?" Sarah asked, taking a bite of her maple bar.

Daniel nodded. "Missions are fun, but I am glad to be back. This one went way longer than I anticipated."

I nodded in agreement. Almost two years ago I had asked Rebecca if she would go on a date with me, and we'd been dating ever since. The same day, Daniel asked Sarah out on a date. I was surprised by how much dating Rebecca changed my perspective. My love of missions and working for Truth Squad was the same, but going on missions without Rebecca was harder than I expected. I wished she could go on every mission with me, and I couldn't wait till her parole ended and she could finally become a Squad Four agent.

After finishing their doughnuts, Rebecca and Sarah got up and headed to their dorm. "See you tomorrow!" Sarah called with a wave.

We waved back. Once they walked out of earshot, Daniel leaned forward. "So, when are you going to ask her?"

I raised my eyebrows. "What?"

"Don't tell me you haven't been planning to ask Rebecca to marry you," Daniel said, crossing his arms with a smirk.

I shrugged, trying to hold back my own grin. "Well, I guess you're right."

"You have the ring already, don't you?"

I rolled my eyes. "How do you figure these things out?"

Daniel smirked. "I've been your friend for a long time. I just know these things."

"Well, I ordered the ring two weeks ago. I designed it myself, so it will take a little longer to be ready."

"Well, it's about time." Daniel winked, then tilted his head. "How'd you find out the ring size?"

"I asked Sarah."

"Do you think they have the same ring size? I might like to know what it is."

"Oh, so you're planning to ask Sarah, too?" I smirked.

Daniel shrugged, his face growing red. "Maybe. So, when are you asking Rebecca?"

I sighed. "I don't know. I'm waiting for the perfect moment, you know?"

Daniel laughed.

"What?" I asked.

He shook his head. "It just cracks me up how different you two are. You fly by the seat of your pants, and Rebecca is super calculated. It's just funny that you two are so different and yet so perfect for each other."

"Well, thank you," I said, doing a fake bow. "And when are you asking Sarah?"

He shrugged. "I don't even have a ring yet, but I'm sure I'll plan a fancy date or something."

"And not wait for the perfect moment?" I teased. "You're so calculated."

Daniel rolled his eyes. "Sure, sure." He glanced at his watch. "It's getting close to midnight, so I'm headed to bed." He stood up and clasped my shoulder. "See you tomorrow."

"Goodnight!" I called as he walked away. I took a deep breath of the night air and closed my eyes, thankful for the end of the mission and being back home.

Lord, thank You for the close of another mission. Thank You for time with friends and for this beautiful evening. Thank You for Rebecca, and help me to find the right time to ask her to marry me. I pray for Your guidance as we navigate this MAX case. My mind drifted away from my prayer to the weird, black box in the file room. *What was that thing?* I wondered. *And what's going on in November?* I shook my head. *Mr. Greyson must have known more than he let on, otherwise he wouldn't have burned all those papers. What did he know about the big plans for November? And why were they so important that he burned everything?*

CHAPTER 2

The next day, I spent the morning tinkering with gadgets in my experimental lab when I got a message from Mr. Truth on my watch. "Come to my office right away."

I set down the camera I was working on and rubbed at the grease on my fingers. *I wonder what's up,* I thought, hurrying out the door.

I hurried to Mr. Truth's office and found it crammed with people. Rebecca, Sarah, Daniel, Matthew, and Mr. Truth were all inside along with Rebecca's parole officer, Agent Brandon, and Agent Holton.

"What's up?" I asked, stepping inside. Rebecca looked nervous, Sarah and Daniel looked just as clueless as I felt, and everyone else looked serious. Something about Mr. Truth's expression, the light in his eyes despite his serious face, made me excited. I grinned. *This must be good.*

"Thanks for coming all of you. These men have some exciting news to share," Mr. Truth said, waving at Agent Brandon and the two officers.

Agent Brandon nodded. "I am pleased to report that the FBI has taken note of the efforts Ms. Sanders has taken on behalf of our nation in aiding certain FBI endeavors." My heartrate picked up and I glanced at Rebecca. Her expression stayed serious. "Ms. Sanders, having taken into account these efforts and the positive reports Mr. Truth has given concerning your parole, we have, in a court of law, explained your case and decreased your parole sentence."

"What?" Rebecca raised her eyebrows.

Agent Brandon nodded. "You heard me. Not only have we decreased your parole, but as of today, based on the signatures of your parole officer and Mr. Truth, you have officially completed it."

Rebecca's jaw dropped. "For real?"

"You mean she's not on parole anymore?" I asked.

"I mean that, based on the court of law, she has served her sentence to the full and is a free woman." Agent Brandon stepped forward and extended his hand.

Rebecca stood up and shook his hand solemnly. Sarah sat in the chair next to her, her hand over her mouth and tears streaming down her face. Daniel placed a hand on Sarah's shoulder and smiled.

I couldn't hold back my excitement. "This is awesome!" I pulled Rebecca into a hug.

"We'll make an announcement to the rest of Squad Four, but we thought this group ought to be the first to hear it," Mr. Truth said. "And, Rebecca?"

"Yes?" She let go of my hug and turned to face him.

"You are now free to take your Squad Four test." He smiled. "Assuming, of course, that you're interested in doing so."

She smiled, a small laugh escaping her lips. "Of course!"

Mr. Truth waved toward the door. "Alright, go celebrate, you all, while I finish up this paperwork."

We hurried out of the building. The moment we stepped outside I jumped up and did a fist-pump. "Yes!"

Rebecca still looked stunned. "I can't believe it."

Sarah hugged her sister, still crying. "I'm so happy! Praise God!"

Daniel nodded. "Yes, praise God!"

Rebecca nodded, a tear slipping out of the corner of her eye. She sighed. I knew that this meant a lot to her. Being on parole was something she bore with a smile, but I knew it was a heavy burden on her heart. Now she could be free from that weight.

"How would you like to celebrate?" I asked, smiling at Rebecca.

"Ice cream and coffee," she said, smiling and wiping away the stray tear. "If you can handle a celebration that doesn't include doughnuts."

"Ice cream is almost as good." I winked. "I think I'll survive."

"That was probably the best affogato I've ever had," Daniel said as we walked out of the ice cream shop. "Also, probably the largest affogato I've ever had. It's a good thing we walked here."

"I know. This shop is the best ever!" I said, grinning.

"It's a nice day to be walking, too," Sarah said, smiling as she glanced up at the sunny, blue sky.

Rebecca's phone dinged and she pulled it out of her pocket, slowing her pace as she read.

"So, what's the plan for the rest of the afternoon?" Daniel asked.

"I'm not sure." I turned to look at Rebecca. She and Sarah had stopped walking and were now a few yards behind us. They looked concerned and were whispering excitedly. "What's up?" I asked, walking back to them.

"Nothing." Rebecca quickly shut off her phone and slid it into her back pocket.

Sarah raised an eyebrow. "Nothing?"

Rebecca ignored her and started walking down the sidewalk again, picking up the pace.

I jogged up to her. "Are you sure it's nothing?" I asked quietly.

She shrugged. "I'm not sure, but I'm not going to make a big deal of it right now. We're supposed to be celebrating." She smiled, almost convincingly.

"Are you able to celebrate very well if you're worrying about something?" I asked, raising my eyebrows. "You might be able to fool us, but I know you won't be all here. Your mind will be on whatever you and Sarah were talking about."

Rebecca didn't respond. She kept her gaze straight ahead and continued walking at her lightning-speed pace.

I sighed. *Lord, whatever is bothering her, help it to turn out okay, and help me to be an encouragement in whatever way I can,* I prayed, not sure what else to pray.

Sarah and Rebecca decided to head to their dorm when we got back to Truth Squad, so our celebration was prematurely over. The rest of the day passed slowly, Daniel and I both wondering what happened as we tinkered with gadgets in the experimental lab. At dinner the twins were still off, Rebecca seeming reserved and Sarah looking anxious. *What would cause this reaction on such a happy day?* I wondered.

The next few days, Daniel and I tried to find out what was going on, but the twins never wanted to talk about it. Finally, we decided to ignore the problem and try to stay positive. "Maybe they'll change their minds eventually," I said hopefully. But nothing seemed to change.

I was leaving the drama classroom at Truth Academy when Rebecca ran up to me holding up a piece of paper, a smile on her face. "Look what I got!"

"What?" I asked, a smile already growing on my face. I grabbed the paper and scanned it. It was a certificate with Rebecca's name on it, and Mr. Truth and Matthew's signatures at the bottom. I looked up at Rebecca. "You passed your Squad Four training?"

She nodded excitedly. "Yes!"

I did a fist-pump and gave her a hug. "Congratulations!" I pulled back and looked her in the eye. "I'm very proud of you."

"Thank you." She smiled, a real smile that wasn't faked.

Maybe she won't be bothered anymore by whatever problem that was, I thought hopefully as we walked out of the classroom building. *Or maybe she'll be willing to talk about it now.*

After dinner, Mr. Truth had the Squad Four ceremony in the chapel, welcoming both Rebecca and one other agent into the Squad Four ranks. I sat in the front of the chapel with Daniel and Sarah. I couldn't keep the smile off my face as Rebecca walked onto the stage, her shoulders square and her expression solemn, but her eyes bright with excitement.

The new members were presented with their uniforms and badges, and then prayed over by the pastor, Mr. Truth, and his wife Mary. After the prayer, the new members were asked to recite and agree to the Truth Squad pledge.

Rebecca recited first, her face glowing as she spoke. "As a member of Truth Squad, I pledge to honor God first and foremost in all I do, to defend the truth at home and abroad, to search for the truth when it is hidden, and to make the truth known, even when no one wants to hear it. I believe that the truth is found in Jesus Christ, and I pledge to stand for the truth no matter the cost." Rebecca finished and looked me in the eye, a small smile pulling at the corners of her mouth.

Once the other member finished reciting the pledge, all the Squad Four members in the building stood and recited the Truth Squad motto and key verse. "Defending the truth across America and throughout the world. 'Sanctify them in the truth; Your word is truth.' John 17:17." I felt a sense of pride swelling in my chest as we spoke in unison, silently thanking God for the opportunity to be a part of Truth Squad, and also thanking Him that Rebecca was finally a Squad Four member.

Mr. Truth turned to face the audience. Smiling, he said, "It is my pleasure to officially announce our newest two members of Squad Four—Rebecca Sanders and Elisha Warren!"

The audience cheered. A full smile broke out on Rebecca's face, warming me up on the inside. I jumped up and did a fist-pump. My cheering was the loudest in the building, and I did not care.

Rebecca joined us as we walked outside after the ceremony. "Everyone who's had trouble telling you two twins apart is going to have even more trouble now that your uniforms match," I said, grinning at Rebecca.

"I'm sure that will come in handy sometimes," she said, winking. Her phone buzzed and she pulled it out of her pocket, her face growing serious.

"What's up?" I asked.

Rebecca shook her head as she looked at her phone. "My brother."

I raised an eyebrow. I knew she had a brother, but she never talked about him besides saying that he lived with her dad growing up. "What's wrong?"

She shook her head. "Nothing." She shoved her phone back in her pocket.

"You're lying," I said, crossing my arms. "You realize we're both special ops agents now, right? I know the signs of lying."

She rolled her eyes. "Look, I just don't know what to make of this. Once my dad left Seattle, I lost touch with both him and my brother. I've changed my cellphone number more times than I can count, so I have no clue how he got my number. And his messages are weird." She shrugged. "It might not even be him. It could be a scam, so as far as I know, it probably is nothing."

I lowered my voice. "If it's nothing, why are you and Sarah so worried about it?"

Rebecca looked down at the ground and kicked at a pinecone. "Because if it is my brother, he might be in trouble."

"So, you're trying to figure out if it's actually him or if it's a scam where someone's trying to steal your money or something?" I asked. Rebecca nodded. "Do you want help? I could try looking up the number to see who it belongs to."

She shrugged. "Did that already. What we found said the number belonged to Isaac Sanders, and that's our brother's name."

"Any other clues as to whether it's him?" I asked.

"Well, the number is a Washington D.C. number, and last I knew, my dad and Isaac lived in Chicago, but that doesn't mean they didn't move again."

"Did you try contacting your dad?"

"He never got back to us." Rebecca sighed. "I really don't want to worry about this right now."

Mr. Truth and Mary walked up and congratulated Rebecca, ending our conversation. Throughout the rest of the evening, I couldn't help thinking about Rebecca's vague responses. *Why does she think Isaac might be in trouble?* I wondered. I knew from the way she was talking, she didn't really think the texts were a scam.

The next day I asked Rebecca if she'd received any new texts from Isaac.

"No," she replied, shrugging.

"What makes you think he's in trouble?" I asked.

Rebecca glared at me. "I thought I told you I didn't want to worry about it."

I crossed my arms. "You said you didn't want to worry about it yesterday. You didn't say I couldn't ask you about it today." I paused and looked Rebecca in the eye. "You seem very concerned about it, and I just want to help."

Rebecca looked down at the ground, her lips pressed tightly together. After a moment of silence, she tensely replied, "I appreciate your concern, but I don't need you to help with anything."

"Well, have you determined if it's actually him?" I asked, trying to keep my voice steady despite my growing irritation.

Rebecca sighed. "Why do you have to keep pushing this?" She paused. "If you have to know, then yes, I'm almost certain that it's actually Isaac."

"How'd you figure it out?" I asked quietly. I felt like I was walking on a minefield, unsure of which question would set off a bomb.

"Sarah and I looked into dad's job in Chicago," she replied slowly. "We found out he was transferred to the company's larger office in Washington D.C. We also found Isaac's social media and saw that he recently graduated from one of the colleges in D.C. and that he got a job at some computer place, and he has a girlfriend." Rebecca raised her eyebrows. "Also, his social media number is the same as the one he's been contacting me with."

"Wow. You did a lot of work then!" I said, impressed. *Or did she know all this yesterday and just didn't tell me?* The thought caught me off-guard, and instantly I felt guilty. *Why are you doubting your best friend?* I inwardly scolded myself. I opened my mouth to ask another question when Sarah called Rebecca's name.

Rebecca glanced over her shoulder at Sarah. "I need to go." She looked back at me. "Luke, please don't be offended. I promise I'll fill you in more when I have more details."

I swallowed back the argument that popped into my head and nodded. "See you later."

Rebecca smiled sympathetically before jogging over to Sarah. I watched as the sisters headed toward the campus entrance, feeling an ache in my heart as they walked away. I wanted to know what was going on, to get in on the action and the problem solving. *Or am I just jealous that she's not letting me in on what's up? That she's only confiding in Sarah, and I wish it was me?* I wondered, turning around. I jumped seeing Daniel standing right behind me.

Daniel laughed. "Sorry, I didn't mean to scare you."

"How long have you been there?" I asked, grinning along with Daniel.

Daniel stopped laughing and looked away, his face growing red.

"You heard that whole conversation, didn't you?"

Daniel shrugged and half-smiled, more like a grimace. "Sorry. I was coming to get you because Mr. Truth needs you to run the Junior training today. I didn't want to interrupt your conversation since it looked pretty serious."

"Well, maybe next time don't eavesdrop," I said, my voice sounding tenser than I intended.

Daniel nodded. "I'm sorry." We stood in awkward silence for a minute. "If it makes you feel any better, I didn't know something was up with the twins' brother, either."

I smiled and shook my head. "Sometimes I do not understand those two. But that kind of does make me feel better."

Daniel grinned. "Good. Now you'd better hurry to the training room. You've got two minutes before the Junior Squad is supposed to start."

The next few days passed in a blur as our squad worked on an emergency mission. With late nights, flights across the country, research, and undercover work filling my time, I forgot about Rebecca's trouble with her brother.

I was headed into Mr. Truth's office with a final report on the mission when I bumped into Rebecca walking out. Her eyes grew wide, and she jumped back. Something was wrong.

"Sorry," she said, trying to dart around me.

"Hold up," I said, trying to step in front of her. She pushed past me and hurried out of the building.

I frowned and hurried into Mr. Truth's office to deliver my report. *Maybe he knows what's up,* I thought.

"Luke," Mr. Truth said as I walked in, his face looking as perplexed as I felt.

"What's up with Rebecca?" I asked, handing him my report.

He shrugged. "I don't know. Actually, I was hoping you knew what was going on."

"What do you mean?"

"Oh, so you don't know?" Mr. Truth asked, raising his eyebrows. I shook my head. "Rebecca just gave her resignation," he said with a sigh.

"What?" My jaw dropped. "Why?"

"I have no clue," Mr. Truth replied, shaking his head. "I was hoping you would know."

I ran out of Mr. Truth's office after Rebecca. She was almost to the girls' dorms. "Rebecca!" I called. She turned her head but kept walking.

I sprinted over to her and stepped in front of her. "Rebecca, what's going on?"

She stopped and stared at the ground. "I resigned," she replied with a shrug, like it was no big deal.

"Why?"

"I needed to." She sighed. "Please just leave me alone and don't follow me."

"What do you mean, 'don't follow you'? Why are you leaving? Where are you going? You can't just leave!" I took a deep breath, running my fingers through my hair. "I thought this was your dream."

"It is!" Rebecca replied, tugging at her braid. "Look, just let me go and then talk with Sarah. Just trust me, please."

The pain in her eyes struck my heart. "Are you in trouble?"

She smiled sadly. "Don't worry about me."

"I'm your boyfriend. I kinda can't help that."

She grabbed my hand and squeezed it. I felt her push a sticky note onto my palm. "Just talk to Sarah. That's all I can say," she whispered.

I gritted my teeth and nodded, knowing the sticky note must say more. *If she has to hand me a sticky note, then someone must be listening in on her, or following her,* I thought, noticing how tense Rebecca's posture was. I slowly let go of Rebecca's hand and stuck my hands in my pockets to discretely push the sticky note into my pocket. "I don't want you to leave," I said honestly.

"I don't want to either," Rebecca said, looking down at the ground.

I knew Rebecca wanted me to walk away and read the note, but I couldn't let her leave without giving her a hug. I pulled her into a bear hug, and whispered, "I love you, and I'll be praying for you."

"Thank you," she whispered back. "Talk to Sarah." She pulled away from my hug and smiled with misty eyes. "See you later."

I nodded and swallowed back the sudden tightness in my throat. "See ya."

I walked to my dorm slowly. Once I was inside, I pulled the sticky note from my pocket. The note was obviously written quickly, as it lacked Rebecca's usually perfect penmanship.

It read: "Luke, this has to do with my brother. Sarah will explain. Put her note with yours to know where to find more info. I can't talk to you because I'm being tracked. Not sure how. See back. Rebecca."

I flipped the sticky note over but didn't see anything. *Probably invisible ink,* I thought, shaking my head. *This message doesn't make much sense on its own. I'd better find Sarah.*

I put the note back in my pocket and headed back outside. I took a couple deep breaths, realizing my heartrate had sped up with my anxiousness for Rebecca. *Lord, this seems really weird,* I prayed as I sent Sarah a message on my watch. *I don't know what's happening with Rebecca, and she can't tell me because she thinks she's being tracked. I want to run after her and protect her, but that might put her in more danger. Lord, please protect her, and give me wisdom.*

Sarah and Daniel met me outside at one of the picnic tables. "Rebecca's gone!" Sarah said, her face pale and her eyes wide. "She barely even told me she was leaving and now she's gone."

Daniel rested a comforting hand on Sarah's shoulder. "What did she take with her?"

"A backpack with her laptop, some clothes, and some gadgets," she replied.

"Did she leave you a sticky note?" I asked, pulling mine out of my pocket.

Sarah nodded and handed hers to me. The note read, "Love you! See back."

"Do either of you have a blacklight pen on you?" I asked, turning the two notes over. "I think there must be an invisible ink message."

Daniel and Sarah shook their heads. "I can go get one from your lab," Daniel offered, and jogged off.

I handed my note to Sarah. "Rebecca said I needed to talk to you to find out what's going on," I said, waiting for her to scan the note.

Sarah took a shaky breath before launching into her explanation. "Rebecca started receiving texts from Isaac recently. At first, they seemed friendly but with each text he added a random letter all by itself. When we put them all together it spelled 'trouble.'"

"That's why Rebecca thought something might be wrong with Isaac," I said.

Sarah nodded. "After we verified that it was actually Isaac messaging her, she tried to send a secret message back to find out what was going on. Instead, she got some message back that was some kind of threat. I didn't see it, but whatever it was convinced her she needed to resign and go find Isaac."

Sarah blinked hard and swallowed before continuing. "I tried to convince her I should go with her, but Rebecca insisted that it would put both her life and Isaac's in danger. Then she told me to talk to you."

"So, you don't really know what's happening either," I said, frustrated. "I guess we need to figure out the secret message to get more info."

Sarah shrugged. "I think that's our only option."

Daniel returned with a blacklight pen and shone it on the sticky notes. Instead of seeing letters like I expected, there were a bunch of lines on each sticky note. Daniel looked perplexed. "I'm not sure how these are supposed to go together."

Sarah took the light from Daniel and started scanning the notes closer. "Ah, here we go," she said, pointing to a corner on one of the notes. A small "L" appeared where she shone the light. "This goes on the left." She looked at the other note, flipping it around until she found a small "R" in one of the corners. "And this one goes like this." She placed the notes next to each other, then held the blacklight up to illuminate the whole picture.

"She drew a picture?" Daniel said, shaking his head. "What is it?"

"It looks like a watch underneath a bed," I said, tilting my head to see the picture correctly. Drawing wasn't Rebecca's strong suit. "Wait, Sarah, was Rebecca wearing her watch when she left?"

Sarah thought for a minute. "I didn't pay attention then, but now that I'm thinking about it, I don't think she had it on."

"So, she must have left information on her watch for us, and her watch must be under her bed," I said, standing up. "Sarah, do you want to go get the watch?"

Sarah nodded and hurried to the girls' dorm building. She returned a few minutes later with the watch. "I found it under my bed instead of hers," she said, handing it to me.

I looked at the recent files on the watch memory storage to see what Rebecca last accessed. It came up with a recent upload. "Looks like there's a document we need to read. Why don't we go to the computer lab so we can read it on a bigger screen?" I grinned. "It would be hard for all three of us to read from a watch."

Sarah and Daniel nodded. We hurried to the computer lab, and once inside I connected the watch to a computer and uploaded the document. Once it loaded, I opened the file, revealing a message from Rebecca followed by several pages of information.

Daniel read Rebecca's message out loud. "Sorry I couldn't talk to you in person, but I'm quite positive I'm being tracked, and I didn't want to do anything that could put my brother in more danger. I believe my brother has been working for MAX and recently tried to defect, and instead of getting rid of him, MAX is using this to get to me. Somehow, I have info he needs, but I don't know what it is. Still something to do with Zaiden's codes, I'm sure."

I nodded, remembering how a couple years ago, MAX had sent an agent to get the codes from Rebecca and assassinate her, but he failed. We never figured out what the codes were needed for, though.

"If you look through the rest of this document, you'll see records of my messages with Isaac as well as one of MAX's agents. Once you read through it, you'll see that Isaac is most definitely working for MAX and it is necessary for me to travel on my own without you. I know I said don't follow me; I'm trusting you aren't. Please take this document to Mr. Truth and follow his advice for what to do next. But don't follow me. Rebecca."

"Wait, does she want us to follow her or not?" Daniel asked, crossing his arms. "I'm so confused."

I hit print on the document and ran over to the printer to grab the paper copy. "She doesn't want us to follow her, but she does want our help," I said, walking back over to the computer.

"How can we help without following her?" Daniel asked, raising an eyebrow.

I lifted the papers. "With this information, I think." I cracked a smile. "I think what she means by this message is that she doesn't want to know if we're following."

Sarah nodded. "I think if we read the rest of the information she's gathered we would have more details, but from her note I would assume that there would be danger in her knowing where we are, or she doesn't want to be connected with us so that she can get in with MAX or something."

"Let's take this to Mr. Truth," I said, hurrying out the door. Moments later we sat in Mr. Truth's office, going through the document. Looking through the text messages, it was obvious that Isaac and the other agent weren't trying to hide their affiliation with MAX. Their messages were very direct, basically threatening harm to Isaac if Rebecca didn't come give them the codes they needed. Rebecca included some maps in the documents, highlighting different meeting points with MAX agents heading across the U.S. to Washington D.C. She had some notes around each of the meeting points, noting that there was a trend of meeting near power plants, except at the meeting point in Washington D.C. "This one doesn't fit the pattern," she wrote next to that spot.

Mr. Truth rubbed his forehead. "This isn't a whole lot to go on."

"But Rebecca is wanting us to follow her, right? That's why she has all these meeting points?" Daniel sighed. "This is weird."

"But she's confident this is leading her to MAX," Mr. Truth said, leaning back in his chair.

I nodded. "While no one ever directly said 'MAX,' they referenced her earlier work with Zaiden and their connection to his boss, so it's got to be MAX."

"Then I'm putting you three on the case," Mr. Truth said, tapping the document. "Do what Rebecca said. Follow her, but don't give away your location to her. We don't want to cause danger to her or her brother, and we also need to find MAX. Things really seem to be heating up with that organization, and this is the only good lead we have."

"It's a stretch at that," Daniel said, tilting his head. "All we have are some meeting points and text messages."

"It's more to go on than what we had before," Mr. Truth argued. "Can you all be ready to go tonight?"

"Yes, sir," I said, standing up.

Mr. Truth stood and shook my hand. "Good. Keep me posted. When we have enough information on MAX, we will send the information to the FBI and work together on what to do next."

We left Mr. Truth's office and I hurried to my dorm to get ready to leave. As I gathered my equipment, I prayed, *Lord, be with us as we go on this mission. Keep Rebecca safe, keep Isaac safe, and help us to find MAX. Give us wisdom and guidance as we work.* I grabbed my Bible off the top of my dresser, bumping my arm on the small box sitting nearby. *Rebecca's ring.* I packed my Bible, then picked up the box, opening it to see the woven gold and silver band studded with small diamonds and rubies and displaying a glittering round diamond. *This is not what I envisioned going on while planning to propose,* I thought with a sigh. I closed the box and stuck it in between my clothes in the suitcase. *I know I need to focus on the mission right now, Lord, but could You please give me a good opportunity to propose? Maybe when this mission ends, and everything goes back to normal?* I zipped up my suitcase and hurried to the hangar.

CHAPTER 3

"You'd think in a town this small we'd be able to find Rebecca easier." Sarah sighed, twisting her hair around her finger.

I nodded, looking around. Five old, dirty pickup trucks and our car were parked on the side of the dusty road, the faded white parking spaces and yellow dotted line down the middle of the street barely visible. "We just need to be patient. I'm sure we'll run into her eventually."

We'd followed the map Rebecca had left, stopping at each highlighted place as we traveled across the U.S. We'd stopped in Idaho, Colorado, Nebraska, and now we were in the middle of nowhere in Indiana. At each stop we barely missed Rebecca. She left some clues at each place, leaving her initials "R. S." at each stop so we knew she'd been there. After missing her again in Nebraska, we decided to skip the meeting place in Missouri and go straight to Indiana. We hoped to beat her there and wait her out; that way we could see what was going on at these meeting places.

"Where do you think she will most likely meet her contact?" Daniel asked. Even though there was a pattern of the highlighted places being near power plants, Rebecca never left a clue near those plants. We found her initials in a coffee shop, a grocery store, carved into a tree... everywhere.

Obviously MAX was trying to keep Rebecca from being easily followed.

"The population of this town is barely over 300," Sarah said, glancing around the few stores lining the street. "I don't think they would meet in any of these stores since the locals would know they were from out-of-town."

"I want to know what they're doing at these meetings," I said, lifting a hand to wave at an old farmer across the road. "Obviously Rebecca knew where each meeting point would be, so if the meetings aren't telling her where to go next, what are the meetings for?"

"Why not go straight to Washington D.C.?" Daniel asked, kicking at a pebble on the sidewalk.

I shrugged. "I guess we'll just wait and find out."

Daniel pointed ahead at a black speck in the distance. "Look, there's a car coming."

We split up, each of us finding a hiding spot where we might be able to see the car as it drove through town. I leaned against the faded yellow wall of the grocery store, waiting for the vehicle to drive by. *It's so flat around here, that car could have been a couple miles away,* I thought.

Eventually I heard the sound of a diesel engine. I glanced around the corner of the building to see a black pickup pull into a parking spot by the feed store. *Maybe it's a farmer,* I thought, waiting to see cowboy boots stepping out of the truck. I got distracted admiring the truck, noticing it was a current model with big tires and a lift kit. A car door slammed, bringing my attention back to the mission. I watched as the truck pulled back onto the road and drove off the way it came. Now that the truck was gone, I could see a small blue car pull out of its parking spot and head down the road towards me. I caught a glimpse of the driver, a heavier woman who looked to be in her forties, and could tell someone else was in the car, but I couldn't see who the passenger was.

Sarah's excited voice came through my earpiece. "We need to follow that blue car!"

"Was that Rebecca in the passenger seat?" I asked, hurrying to where we'd parked our vehicle.

"Yes. Didn't you see? That truck pulled up and a second later the blue car pulled up. Rebecca hopped from one vehicle to the other and then they sped off." Sarah and Daniel got to our vehicle the same time I did. "That must be why they're meeting. They're switching cars in each state," Sarah finished.

I hopped into the passenger seat of the car while Daniel took the driver's seat and Sarah jumped in the back. "Let's hurry up and follow, then!"

As we sped down the road, Daniel glanced over at me, raising an eyebrow. "Got distracted by the truck?" he asked.

I rolled my eyes. "You have to admit, it was pretty awesome looking. I was expecting to see a cool farmer jump out of that thing."

Daniel grinned. "Same."

"Boys and their trucks. Good thing I was here to pay attention," Sarah scolded, but I could hear the smile in her voice.

We caught up to the blue car after a few minutes, and Daniel slowed down to keep our distance. We didn't want them to know they were being followed. We drove for several hours behind the blue car, slowly moving into more populated areas. Eventually we hit Indianapolis, as well as evening traffic.

"This traffic is insane!" Daniel said as a semitruck pulled in front of us. "Can anyone see the car?"

I pressed my face against my window, trying to see around the truck. "Nope."

"We lost them again?" Sarah's voice was mixed with fear and frustration.

"Don't give up too easily," I said, trying to sound enthusiastic. "This truck will move out of the way in no time, I'm sure."

A half hour later I regretted those words as we sat behind the same truck, barely inching forward every other minute. "Maybe we should find a parking spot and run ahead. It would probably be faster at this point," I said, glancing out the window as a hitchhiker shuffled past our car.

Daniel nodded. "True. They've got to be sitting in this traffic somewhere up ahead."

"Unless they turned off somewhere," Sarah said. She rested her chin in her hands. "The road split not too far back, and before that there were several turns they could have made to go through downtown instead of through this pass."

I looked back out the front windshield, suppressing the sigh that was building up inside me. *Why did we have to hit rush-hour traffic?*

After a few minutes of silence, Daniel cleared his throat. "If they turned off at another point, we should meet back up with them eventually if we keep heading to the next meeting point on Rebecca's map."

I cracked a smile while inwardly scolding myself for being a worrywart. "Brilliant thinking, Mr. Detective," I said in my best British accent.

Daniel grinned. "Thanks. Now, would one of you two put the destination in the GPS?"

Sarah grabbed the map from the folder of Rebecca's notes and found the next meeting point. "Looks like we're headed to Charleston, West Virginia."

I smiled as I entered the destination in the GPS, remembering a thousand comedy bits about West Virginia, but decided to keep them to myself. "Three-hundred and ten miles to go."

"Plenty of time to catch up with Rebecca," Sarah replied with a yawn.

It was midnight by the time we reached Charleston. We caught back up with the blue car along the way, and once we were in Charleston, Rebecca was dropped off at a hotel. I watched as Rebecca walked inside and the blue car drove away. "Why are they just dropping her off?" I asked, utterly confused.

"Is Rebecca just taking a bunch of Uber rides? Is she not actually meeting with any contacts?" Sarah asked, rubbing her forehead.

"Would it hurt anything for us to go ask her what's up?" I wondered.

Daniel glanced at me, his eyebrows raised. "Do I even need to answer that?"

I shrugged, knowing it probably would cause problems considering Rebecca's insistence that she not know she was being followed. "Okay, so we probably shouldn't stay in the same hotel as Rebecca, since we're trying to avoid being spotted by her."

Sarah looked up another place for us to stay, and once there we sent Mr. Truth an update on where we were and how things were going. "I wish we had more info to send," I told Daniel after clicking send on the message.

Daniel nodded. "I'm sure we'll have more soon. This is the last stop before Washington D.C. Once we're there, I'm sure we'll learn a lot more about what's going on."

I nodded, hopeful that he was right. *Lord, please keep Rebecca safe, and help us to be helpful from a distance.*

I had trouble sleeping that night, wondering why this mission felt so different from other missions. While every mission had dangerous elements to it, moments of stress and frustration and having no clue what was going on, there was something different about this mission. *Is it because we're trying to find MAX, or is it because of Rebecca?* I wondered. *Or both?*

We got up at five the next morning and waited outside the hotel to find out where Rebecca was headed. Around six o'clock Rebecca headed out the door with her backpack on and started walking toward the Kanawha River.

"Luke, why don't you follow her on foot," Daniel said as he started the car. "Keep your coms in and give us updates on what's going on. But remember to keep your distance." He gave me a seriously-don't-get-distracted look.

"Of course I'll remember," I replied, dramatically placing a hand over my heart. "Whatever makes you doubt me?"

Daniel rolled his eyes and pulled out of the parking spot. He drove down the road a ways and dropped me off on the sidewalk a little past where Rebecca was walking.

After giving a quick salute, I jumped from the car with my backpack and sunglasses on and headed toward the river. I took out my smartphone and faked taking selfies until I saw Rebecca hurry past. Once she was far enough away, I stopped faking the selfies and began following her, keeping my distance like I promised Daniel. I glanced around as I walked, noticing the amount of orange and red leaves on the trees. Coming from Oregon, I was used to seeing mostly pine trees instead of mostly deciduous trees. *This is a pretty place,*

I thought, enjoying the moment before Daniel buzzed in my ear asking where I was headed.

After walking for twenty minutes, Rebecca strolled into a coffee shop next to the river. "She just entered a little coffee shop," I told Daniel, looking at the sign by the road. "Coffee and Cakes."

Before entering the coffee shop, I grabbed a jacket and baseball cap from my backpack and put them on. The jacket was Daniel's, not mine, and it was brand new, so I hoped it would help me stay invisible to Rebecca. The baseball cap was for a football team I didn't care about, so I figured that would help with the disguise, too.

I opened the door to the coffee shop and stepped inside, altering my gate to a lazier appearance, sticking my hands in my pockets as I stepped into the line to order. I glanced around the room to locate Rebecca, knowing my gaze would be hidden behind my reflective sunglasses. I spotted her at a two-person table, sitting up perfectly straight with her arms folded on the table in front of her. She kept glancing at her watch and looking around, her facial expression perfectly calm. *She's waiting for someone,* I thought as I stepped forward in line.

There was something about Rebecca's stellar acting skills and her critical thinking that always brought a smile to my face, and I had to work hard to hold back my smile. Even though we worked in the same field at Truth Squad, we were super different in our working styles which seemed to go well together.

After quietly placing my order under the fake name "Jerry," and making sure to order coffee cake instead of a doughnut so as not to alert Rebecca, I found a place to sit at the bar-height table behind Rebecca. The table had charging outlets for laptops which was perfect for my cover, and sitting behind Rebecca meant I had a greater chance of not being discovered by her.

I set up my laptop and placed my fingers on the keys, not bothering to type since no one was sitting next to me. "Rebecca is sitting at a table, and she looks like she's waiting for someone," I whispered into my coms. I heard the barista call "Jerry" and sauntered over to the counter. As I grabbed my coffee and cake, I heard the bell over the door ring. Out of the corner of my eye I watched Rebecca stand up and nod.

I slowly walked back to my table, wanting to rush so I could see who Rebecca was meeting with, but knowing that would blow my cover. After setting down my coffee and settling in front of my laptop, I looked up over the edge of the screen at Rebecca's contact.

"Rebecca's contact is here," I said into my coms. I studied the face of the dark-haired girl who sat across from Rebecca, feeling like I knew her from somewhere. She had a lot of attitude. Suddenly, it clicked. "I recognize her. It's Lisa, her old co-worker."

"Really?" Sarah replied, her voice pitching up in surprise. "Didn't she get caught when Zaiden's operation was taken down?"

"I don't know. Maybe you should look into that." Rebecca and Lisa appeared to be deep in conversation, Lisa looking frustrated about whatever Rebecca was saying. *Just like old times,* I thought, remembering that they never got along well.

A few minutes later, Rebecca got up and left. Lisa sat for a few more minutes before leaving the shop. I filled Daniel and Sarah in on what just happened as I put my laptop away. "Follow Lisa," Sarah said through the coms. "Daniel can keep tabs on Rebecca, and I'll monitor your progress."

I hurried out the door and followed Lisa down the street. I pulled off my sunglasses so I could see better in the cloudy weather. I was surprised by the number of people out and about at this time of morning until I remembered that people were probably headed to work. Lisa walked briskly, weaving in and out of people. She reached a crosswalk and jogged across the road. By the time I caught up, the light had changed, and I was stuck waiting. After what felt like forever, the light turned red, and the walk light flashed for the crosswalk.

"I think I lost her," I said as I ran across the street. I jogged down the sidewalk, looking for a familiar face. As I passed the door to a small boutique, it slammed open and hit my arm.

"Sorry," the lady said as she stepped out the door. We made eye-contact.

Lisa!

Her eyes widened and she took off running. I ran after her.

"Just ran into Lisa. Literally. I think she recognized me," I said, darting between people as I chased after her.

"We can't let her get back to MAX knowing that we're following Rebecca. You've got to catch her," Sarah said.

"Copy that." I followed Lisa down a side alley, dodging trashcans.

"Daniel is nearby. I'll send him your coordinates," Sarah said.

I picked up my pace, noticing Lisa was slowing. The advantage of my height and long stride was paying off. About three yards away from her I called, "Lisa!" She looked over her shoulder, her eyes widening as she picked up her pace.

Daniel darted into view on the other side of the alley, blocking Lisa's path. "Stop right there."

Lisa stopped and took a few steps back, then turned around to face me. "I knew I recognized you. Rebecca said she was on her own!" she said angrily.

"She is," I replied. "Now, we both know Truth Squad has evidence to turn you in, so you can either surrender and give us some info, or just be turned in." I grinned. "And as you probably know, surrendering usually goes better in court. So, it's your choice."

"I choose neither." Lisa whipped a gun from behind her back. Daniel flew into action as I ducked behind a dumpster to avoid Lisa's shot. Daniel grabbed Lisa's wrist and twisted the gun from her grip.

I jumped out of my hiding spot and grabbed the gun from the ground. "Sarah, are you getting all this?" I asked into my coms.

"Affirmative. I've sent the information to headquarters. Stand by while you wait for the police," Sarah replied in typical business fashion.

"Okay, so, while we wait for the police—"

Lisa jumped in, interrupting me. "It's too late."

I raised an eyebrow. "Too late for what?"

"You won't get any helpful information from me. It won't matter. Rebecca told you not to follow her and you did anyways. And now MAX knows." Lisa pressed her lips together and shrugged. "You should have known better."

My heart skipped a beat, and I took a deep breath to calm myself. "I told you Rebecca is working alone."

"Doesn't matter. Don't care if she's gone solo or if she's undercover for your silly organization. The fact that you're following her is a threat, and I reported it." She tilted her chin up proudly.

For not wanting to give helpful information, she seems pretty helpful to me, I thought, holding back a laugh. "That was a pretty quick report," I said, choosing my words carefully. *She has to have coms - she wouldn't have had time for any other kind of report. I need to be careful what I say.*

49

Lisa clamped her jaw shut, and I knew I said the wrong thing. *Now we won't get any more info,* I thought, disappointed in myself.

The police showed up a few minutes later, and we got word from Mr. Truth that another Truth Squad agent would fill out the necessary paperwork for us. "Keep going with the mission," Mr. Truth said.

"It's going to be risky now that MAX knows Rebecca is being followed," Daniel said.

"I know." Mr. Truth said. "But we've got to take the risk. We need to know what's going on with MAX. I have a feeling if we don't act soon, we'll be in for a big disaster."

I swallowed, trying to hold back the argument that popped into my head. *He's right,* I told myself. *This is bigger than just keeping Rebecca safe, although that's important. Something's going down with this MAX thing in November, and Rebecca's going to lead us to it.* I forced a smile after my inner pep-talk. *Let's do this.*

After a quick search, we had to face the fact that we'd lost Rebecca. Again. "I guess we're back to trying to beat her to the next meeting point," Daniel said with a shrug.

"Washington D.C.," Sarah said, biting her lip. "I was sure hoping we could learn more information about MAX before we got there."

"Me too," I said, nodding. I offered to drive this leg of the trip, both so that Daniel could have a break and so that I would have something to keep my mind engaged with besides worrying about Rebecca.

After a couple hours of driving, we got a notification from Mr. Truth. "Looks like we've got some more info from Lisa," Sarah said, reading the message. "First off, Mr. Truth looked into Lisa and the Zaiden case. Somehow, she got bailed out of jail and disappeared. No one has been able to locate her since."

"Weird," I said, raising an eyebrow.

"Yeah. So, Mr. Truth said she admitted to working for MAX. She also hasn't met the boss, but he has a lot of activity in D.C., so she thinks his headquarters are there." Sarah paused. "Um, she said she was sent to deliver a message to Rebecca, but she doesn't know what it is and even if she did, she wouldn't tell us." Sarah shook her head and looked up from the message. "She probably knows a lot more than she said."

"She probably also thinks she only shared info we already know, which could be true," Daniel said. "Although she confirmed our suspicions about a headquarters in D.C."

I nodded. "But she doesn't know for sure. Also, I'm guessing she doesn't really know why Rebecca is involved, and her comment about not knowing the message is probably true."

"Why do you think that?" Sarah asked.

"Because Lisa and Rebecca were always at odds with each other, and I would guess that she would enjoy dishing out what she knows if she thought it would get Rebecca in trouble," I explained. "At least, that's my theory. Lisa seemed kind of frustrated with Rebecca at the coffee shop. I wouldn't be surprised if she delivered the message and wanted to know what it was, and Rebecca wouldn't tell her."

Daniel smirked. "Sounds like something the two of them would do."

We were silent for a couple of minutes. "So, what do we do when we get to D.C.? Do you think Lisa actually contacted someone?" Sarah asked, sounding worried.

Daniel slowly opened his mouth. "Um, there's a good chance she did," he replied quietly. "Did Mr. Truth's report mention whether she had coms or not?"

Sarah scanned the message again. "Yes, she did."

"Then she probably told somebody," I said, trying to sound nonchalant. "But she said she's never met the boss, so we know the message didn't get directly to him." *Yet.*

"Maybe she told whoever was picking up Rebecca today," Daniel suggested.

I nodded. "If that's the case, then maybe Rebecca can convince them she's not being followed, or that if she is, she can lose us."

Sarah shrugged. "I hope that's the case. Rebecca can be pretty convincing."

I hope so too, I thought, not wanting to think of any alternatives to who Lisa may have contacted. *But what if the news has reached the boss already? What then?*

CHAPTER 4

"I think we're stuck." Daniel glanced around at the mass of vehicles and people in Washington D.C. "There's no way we can find Rebecca in this mess."

"Finding a needle in a haystack doesn't hold a candle to finding an agent in this city," I said, trying to lighten the mood.

Sarah smiled politely at my attempted humor. "We've got to find a way to track her location."

"I know you said she took a laptop with her. Does she have her smartphone on her, or did she leave that behind?" I asked.

"I'm not sure about the smartphone," Sarah said. "But I think you have a good idea. If she has her smartphone, you could track that."

"And if she doesn't, we could try tracking the laptop, but that might be harder," I said.

We got a hotel room with a kitchenette and set it up to be our own headquarters. I got my laptop out and got to work tracking Rebecca's phone. *Please, Lord, let her phone be on her and not back at Truth Squad,* I prayed as the program ran its search.

Daniel elbowed me, jerking my attention away from the screen. "Relax, dude," he said, a slight grin on his face.

"What makes you think I'm not relaxed?" I said, faking a yawn and stretching my arms exaggeratedly.

"Hmm, maybe the lack of chatter while you wait for the scan to run, or the fact that you haven't asked for doughnuts yet. Not sure which." Daniel shrugged.

I grinned. "Now that you mention it..."

"Oh, no." Daniel face-palmed. "Why did I say anything?"

"Maybe we should get some doughnuts." Before Daniel could reply, my laptop beeped. I turned to look at the scan results. Rebecca's smartphone location had been tracked to a suburb of Washington D.C. "Yes! We have a lead!" I said, doing a fist-pump.

"Great!" Sarah said, walking over to us. She looked at the map showing the smartphone's location, then glanced at us. "What's the plan now?"

We thought silently for a moment. "One of us could go to this location and start tracking Rebecca," Daniel suggested.

"Once we find her, we could take turns tracking," I added. "That way we can always have one person tracking and one person staying in contact with them while the third person can rest."

"Sounds like a good plan to me," Sarah said, nodding. "Who wants to track down the phone?"

The three of us exchanged awkward eye-contact for a couple seconds. I shrugged. "I'm up for it."

Daniel gave a thumbs-up. "Great. I'll track your location for now, then if you need to switch I'll take your place and Sarah can take mine."

"Cool." I grinned. "Let's do this."

Not long later I was driving through D.C. traffic, wishing Rebecca's final meeting location with MAX was in a less populated area. Rebecca's smartphone was located in North

Potomac, which was supposed to be a thirty-minute drive away. Due to the notorious rush-hour D.C. traffic, I was in North Potomac fifty minutes after leaving the hotel.

"Alright, I'm here," I said into my coms. I turned into a neighborhood and parked along the side of the road, glancing around at the number of brick houses lining the streets, mentally comparing them to the mostly wood, vinyl, and composite sided homes in Oregon.

"It looks like Rebecca may have changed locations slightly," Daniel said. "I'm sending new coordinates to your watch."

A second later my watch vibrated. The new coordinates showed that the smartphone location was now at a recreation center instead of in this neighborhood. I entered the coordinates into the GPS and started the car again.

Ten minutes later I pulled into a parking spot at the recreation center. "It looks like the location is on the left side of the building. I'd check outside before checking inside," Daniel said.

"Copy that." I hopped out of the car and walked to the left side of the building, noticing how dark it was getting outside. There was a dumpster, one small door, and very few windows on this side of the building.

"You're pretty much on it," Daniel said.

"Really?" I glanced around. I was the only one there. I felt a sinking feeling in my stomach as I stared at the dumpster. *She probably dumped her phone here,* I thought, walking over to it. I opened the lid and saw only two full garbage bags inside. I got down and looked underneath the dumpster. It was too dark to see. I grabbed my phone from my pocket and dialed Rebecca. The light of an incoming call flashed underneath the dumpster. *Yup. She dumped her phone.* I reached under the dumpster, stretching until I could touch the phone and slide it closer to myself.

"Sir, are you okay?" I heard a voice ask behind me.

I looked up to see a lady with a green shirt that read "staff" standing there, holding a trash bag. She raised an eyebrow skeptically.

"Yes, ma'am, I just dropped something under the dumpster," I said, pulling the phone out and sliding it into my back pocket as I stood up.

The employee slowly walked over to the dumpster and threw the trash bag inside, not taking her eyes off me. Finally, she shrugged. "Whatever you say."

"Have a nice day," I replied cheerfully as she backed over to the door. I turned and hurried to my car, not wanting to cause any more suspicions with this employee.

I sighed as I started the car. I pressed the power button on Rebecca's smartphone and noticed that the screensaver picture was generic rather than her usual selfie with Sarah. I swiped to unlock the screen. It opened. *That's not normal,* I thought, knowing she usually had a password she would change every year for security. I checked the phone memory. *Empty.* I sighed, a small growl escaping from my throat.

"Did you find it?" Daniel asked.

"Yes." I tossed the phone onto the passenger seat and started driving. "She dumped her phone under the dumpster. It's empty."

"Wait, did you say under the dumpster?" Sarah piped up.

"Yeah. Why?"

"Why would her phone be under the dumpster instead of inside it? She must have wanted you to find it."

"But Sarah, it was empty," I replied, pulling onto the main road. "I'm coming back to the hotel unless either of you have a better idea."

Daniel sighed. "No, it seems like we're back to square one."

I drove in silence for a few minutes, praying for a new lead, or at least some new ideas. "I guess you and Sarah could start tracking Rebecca's laptop."

"On it," Daniel said. I heard computer keys clicking. "Oh, since you're out driving, do you want to pick up some dinner before coming back?"

"No problem."

With the traffic and a detour through a fast-food drive-thru, it was nine o'clock by the time I got back to the hotel. I hurried back to the room and set down the milkshake tray and three meal bags on the table. "Have you found any trace of Rebecca yet?" I tossed Rebecca's empty phone onto the table beside the milkshakes.

"Ooh, milkshakes!" Sarah said, walking over to the table. She grabbed the chocolate milkshake, and I noticed her slip Rebecca's phone into her pocket.

"Thanks for picking up dinner," Daniel said. "We're still running a scan for the laptop, so no leads yet."

"Seriously?" I ran my fingers through my hair. *Why does it have to take so long? And why did she dump her phone? That was our only way of following her, and now we're stuck!*

Daniel clasped my shoulder. "Just be patient, dude. I'm sure we'll find a lead once the scan finishes running." He grabbed a milkshake and opened a bag of waffle fries and a fried chicken sandwich. "Let's eat and then see how the scan is going."

We prayed for the meal and ate in relative silence. I finished my sandwich and fries quickly, then took my strawberry milkshake over to the computer to check on the progress. The progress bar showed only 27% completion on the scan. "Man, this is going to take forever," I moaned.

Sarah nodded. "Since she dumped her phone, Rebecca's probably using burner phones which won't do us much good.

And we have her watch she left at Truth Squad, so we can't track that. What else could we track?"

Daniel shook his head. "I don't know."

"Have you tried traffic cams yet?" I asked.

"I'm not sure it's time to pull that just yet," Daniel said, giving me the look. "I don't feel right about hacking that, and we currently don't have a missing persons case, either."

I sighed and glanced at the ground, praying for patience. "So, what next?"

Daniel glanced at his watch. "I'm not sure there's much more we can do tonight. All we can do is wait for the scan to finish running and go from there in the morning." He glanced between Sarah and me. "Don't worry. We'll find her."

Sarah and I nodded. "Let's pray," I said.

"Sure." We bowed our heads and Daniel prayed. "Lord, we pray for Your hand to guide us to where Rebecca is. Help us to find a lead so that we can help Rebecca in the best way we can. We also pray for wisdom as we work on the MAX case. Expose what's going on and keep us safe as we investigate. We pray for a good night's rest, too, and peace so that we can have clear minds as we work. We trust You. In Jesus' name, amen."

We chatted for a few minutes, then decided to call it an early night. "I'll stay up for a little while longer," Sarah said. "I have something I want to work on, and I'll keep an eye on the scan, too."

As Daniel and I left, I glanced out of the corner of my eye to see Sarah pull Rebecca's phone from her pocket. *Does she think she'll find some clues on the phone? How will she find anything when the memory is empty?* I wondered.

I woke up early the next morning, and after getting ready for the day went to the kitchen to check on the scan for Rebecca's laptop. The scan was at 90% and still hadn't found anything. *Rats.* I noticed a folded piece of paper sitting next to Rebecca's phone. I grabbed the paper and unfolded it. The paper had a few hearts and flowers doodles across the top. The first three rows had random symbols and shapes. The rest of the paper had a random bunch of words that read almost like a kid making up a story, one that's kind of funny but makes no sense.

"What's that?"

I jumped at Daniel's voice. "Dude, you scared me!"

He grinned. "Sorry about that."

I handed him the paper. "This was folded up next to Rebecca's phone. I'm assuming Sarah wrote this."

Daniel nodded. "That looks like her doodling, anyway."

"But what does it mean?" I asked, crossing my arms. "Like, is this stuff she found on Rebecca's phone? If so, then I have some questions."

Daniel nodded. "Like what's with the weird story?"

"Yeah, and the symbols. And how did she find anything on the phone when the memory was empty?" I grinned. "Or maybe she was writing in her sleep, and that's why it makes no sense."

"Are you talking about me?" Sarah asked, walking into the kitchen. She blinked a few times and yawned. "I don't sleepwalk, by the way."

"Are you sure? 'Cause this note could prove you wrong," I said with a sly grin.

She sat down at the table and yawned again. "I'm sure. I found that on Rebecca's phone."

"Really? But the memory was empty. Where'd you find it?" I asked.

"The message was on a piece of paper inside the phone case," Sarah replied, popping the phone case off and pulling out a small square of paper. "The symbols were on the notes app. Apparently, the phone memory wasn't completely empty, or maybe she did something to make the phone say it was empty when it wasn't."

"Why would she have this weird message on her phone?" Daniel asked, shaking his head. "Does she have a key for these messages?"

Sarah smiled. "Well, I'm the key for the story."

"What?" Daniel and I replied in unison.

Sarah nodded. "That's a secret code Rebecca and I invented when we were little."

"What about the symbols? Can you decipher that, too?" I asked.

She shook her head. "No. I was hoping I could find a key to that somewhere on her phone, but so far, I haven't." She yawned again. "I stayed up pretty late trying to figure that one out."

"Well, what does the story mean?"

"She explained that she dumped her phone because her contact knew she was being followed, and she knew that was the only way we could follow her," Sarah said.

"Wait, does that mean she doesn't think we can track her laptop?" I crossed my arms.

Sarah shrugged. "That or she wants her contact to think so." Sarah read the paper again before continuing. "She said she has some leads on MAX but can't contact us just yet, and she said to use the other message to find what area she'll be in."

"So, we have to know what the symbols and shapes mean to find Rebecca," Daniel said. "I guess we'd better get to work decoding that, then." Daniel laughed as Sarah yawned again. "Maybe we should make a coffee run," he joked.

"I can do that," I offered. "There's a coffee shop a couple blocks over I saw when I was driving yesterday. Let me guess, two caramel lattes?" I grabbed the car keys.

Sarah nodded and Daniel gave me a thumbs-up. "We'll work on decoding this while you're gone," he said.

I decided to drive to the coffee shop since carrying three coffee cups for a few blocks sounded like a bad idea. I walked inside the quaint local shop and ordered two caramel lattes and a maple pecan latte for myself. As I waited for the coffees I glanced around the shop, noting the distressed wood on the front counter, the black metal shelves for the coffee syrups, a local artist's work for sale, and the copper chandelier with old-fashioned Edison lightbulbs. Most coffee shops stuck to a modern, minimalist look, so this blast-from-the-past made the shop stand out. *Rebecca would love this shop,* I thought as my name was called.

I grabbed the coffee tray, thanked the barista, and headed out the door. I stepped outside and held the door open for a couple walking in. As I let go of the door, my eyes met a familiar face heading toward me. *Rebecca!* I nodded and stepped to the side of the sidewalk as she and a man next to her walked past me. Despite my urge to turn and follow Rebecca, I walked in the opposite direction toward the car. As I unlocked the car and opened the door, I looked over my shoulder down the sidewalk. Rebecca and that guy were still in sight, the man looking over his shoulder several times. I hopped in the car and called Daniel on my smartphone.

I pulled out of my parallel parking space and headed down the road as Daniel answered the call. "I found her," I said excitedly before Daniel could even say hello.

"Really?"

"Yes! She and some dude were walking down the sidewalk as I left the coffee shop. Should I follow her?" I asked, hoping he would say yes since I already decided I would.

"Well, I'm sure I don't have the option to say no, knowing you," Daniel replied.

I grinned. *Nope.* As I drove past Rebecca and her companion, I tried to get a good look at the guy's face in my rearview mirror. Luckily, the intersection light was red, so I had a little time. He was the same height as Rebecca, had dark hair and a goatee, and he wore a fancy business suit with a red tie. His arms looked huge. *Probably a body builder. If my muscles are guns, then his are cannons.*

"Do you have your earpiece on you? Do you have a tracking device to plant on Rebecca or this other guy? Is following them right now really going to be helpful?" Daniel asked, sounding skeptical.

"Well, I don't think I have an earpiece, but I'll see if we have a tracker somewhere in the car," I replied, driving down the road a few blocks before turning on a side street and parking. I searched the glove compartment for a tracking device. "You or Sarah could run down here and bring a tracking bug," I said as I climbed into the backseat to keep looking.

"Will we have time for that?" Daniel asked. I heard movement on his end of the phone, so I assumed he was getting a tracking bug.

"Sure. I'll keep following them on foot and you bring the tracking bug. I think Sarah should stay to monitor progress since she doesn't have time to put on a disguise," I said. I grabbed my Bluetooth earbuds from the glove compartment and connected my phone. *That will have to do for my earpiece for now.*

I hopped out of the car and hurried to find Rebecca and her companion. I didn't see them anywhere on the main road sidewalks. *Why are they here, of all places?* I wondered, glancing into shop windows as I passed. *And where did they go?* I prayed they hadn't gotten into a car and driven off while I was searching for a tracking bug. I stopped at a crosswalk, and as I waited for the signal light to change, I saw Rebecca and the dude walk out of a shop and head back the other direction.

"What's your ETA?" I asked Daniel, sprinting across the street when the light changed.

"Just got to the main street. Where are you?"

I glanced at the store next to me. "Just passed Eddie's Bakery. Headed south."

A second later Daniel jogged up to me, breathing heavy. "Since I'm here, we might as well work together." He pulled a tracker from his pocket. "You hanging onto this or am I?"

"You hang onto it. That guy she's with seemed suspicious of me, so I think you need to be the one to plant the tracker," I replied.

"Got it." Daniel pulled an earpiece from his pocket and handed it to me. "That will be easier than talking on the phone."

I nodded, pulling out my earbuds and replacing them with the earpiece. "I'll keep tracking them. You try to get ahead of them so you can brush past Rebecca."

"Sounds good." We checked our coms, then Daniel hurried off down a side street.

I continued following Rebecca, keeping about half a block of distance between us so that hopefully they wouldn't know I was following them. "Try to get to the parking garage at the end of the street and walk out from there," I told Daniel, seeing the concrete building up ahead. "You'll have to be fast though."

"Okay," Daniel replied, breathing heavily.

I kept following Rebecca and the dude when suddenly they split up. "Daniel, the guy just turned into a store, but Rebecca is still headed your way."

"Should I try to talk to Rebecca?" Daniel asked between breaths.

"I don't know. It could be risky," I replied, wondering why they split up.

I walked past the store the big dude had walked into, glancing into the windows. I didn't see him inside. Suddenly, I felt someone grab the back of my shirt and pull me into a small alley between shops. "Whoa, let me go," I said, trying not to overdo my reaction. Two beefy hands whirled me around to face the guy who had been walking with Rebecca. *Oh, boy,* I thought.

"You followin' us?" the man asked with a growl.

"No," I said, trying to act surprised and intimidated. I knew I could get out of this guy's grasp with a few martial arts moves Truth Squad training had taught me, but I also knew if I played scaredy-cat, I might get some info from him.

"We ran into you outside that coffee shop, you drove off, and now you're walkin' along behind us. Sounds like followin' us to me." He tightened his grip and shook me.

"Okay, okay, I was..." I paused as Daniel's voice rang in my earpiece.

"What's going on, Luke? Do you need help?"

I need an excuse fast. I can't let him discover the earpiece, I thought. "I was..."

"Spill it!" the guy said, shaking me again.

"I was going to ask that chic for her number," I replied quickly. The guy looked mad. *Oh, no. That was the wrong answer.* "But I think I know better than that now," I said, making my voice shake. *Now get off my case please.*

The man pushed me back against the wall and let me go. "She's my girl and you can't have her number. Now leave!" He pointed out of the alley.

"Sure, sure, just take it easy," I said, slowly backing away. I turned and ran down the street back toward my car. After a block, I turned into another alley.

"Luke, what's going on?" Daniel asked.

"That dude spotted me trailing them and pulled me aside for an interview," I replied.

"Did you get any useful information?"

"Not really." I walked down the alley to the back side of the businesses and headed toward the parking garage. "Did you plant the tracker? And since I was distracting the big guy, were you able to talk to Rebecca?"

"Yes to both. Why don't you pick me up with the car and let's head back? If that guy's suspicious of you, we don't want to stick around and make things worse."

I sighed. "You're right." I turned around and headed back to the car. *Why'd I have to be stuck talking to the big guy while Daniel got to talk to Rebecca?* I thought, frustrated. I knew the choice to split up the way we had was the best one to have made, but my desire to talk to Rebecca felt like it was winning the battle over my logic. *Especially after that guy called Rebecca his girl. She's not his girl. She's my girl!* The urge to punch that guy in the nose was welling up in me.

I picked up Daniel and drove back to our hotel "HQ." We reheated our now lukewarm coffees in the microwave while Daniel filled us in on the little he'd learned from Rebecca.

"She said we're following too close, and her contacts are getting suspicious. She wants us to loosen up on trailing her," Daniel said.

"Did she let you give her the tracking bug, then?" Sarah asked, crossing her arms.

"She put it inside the hood of her jacket."

The microwave beeped and I pulled out our coffees. "So, unless she wears the jacket every day, that will only be sort of helpful," I said. *If she's wanting us to loosen up on tracking her, there's no way she'll be wearing that jacket every day,* I thought. We sat down at the table. "Learn anything interesting from the tracking bug so far?" I asked Sarah.

Sarah glanced at the laptop and shrugged. "She seems to be staying in the area. Looks like after you and Daniel left, Rebecca and her contact drove about five miles west into a residential area."

"Well, if the tracker doesn't move much, then maybe that's where Rebecca is staying," Daniel suggested.

I nodded. We silently sipped our coffees for a minute, Sarah occasionally glancing at the laptop. "So," I said, drawing out the word. "What's the plan now? How do we loosen up on tracking Rebecca while keeping tabs on her?"

Daniel leaned back in his chair and rubbed his forehead. "Maybe we should wait and see whether the tracker moves. If it doesn't, we could go investigate the location."

Sarah nodded. "That at least gives us something to go on instead of running around like chickens with our heads cut off."

"We should probably avoid both of those things—being chickens and having our heads cut off," I said with a smirk.

Daniel chuckled. "Way to make it weird, dude."

I tilted my chin and nodded dramatically. "My specialty."

CHAPTER 5

After ten minutes, the tracker began moving again. After some time, it stopped moving, back in the same area I'd found Rebecca's phone. "Do you think she dumped the jacket, too?" Daniel asked, glancing between Sarah and me.

Sarah shook her head. "That wouldn't make sense to dump her jacket in the same place she dumped her phone." She paused. "Unless she was trying to give us some sort of clue."

"Speaking of clues, did you get the clue she left in her phone decoded?" I asked.

She shook her head. "I've looked up a few different legends, but nothing makes sense."

"Well, if we decode the clue and the location matches where Rebecca's tracker is, we'll know we've got our location down," I said. "Can I see the clues?"

Sarah nodded and handed me the papers. The bigger paper was Sarah's rewritten clue with the doodles and symbols at the top. The smaller piece of paper was the one from inside Rebecca's phone case, written in extremely small handwriting. *Impressive,* I thought, wondering if Rebecca had used a magnifying glass to write this small.

Sarah and Daniel started talking about the location of Rebecca's tracker. *North Potomac.* I counted the symbols on

Sarah's notes. *Thirteen symbols and no repeats. North Potomac has twelve letters and several repeats. Rats!* I sighed. *Why can't she just be a little clearer?*

I tried to suppress my growing frustration with Rebecca and looked back at her handwritten clue again. The word "out" caught my eye, and I noticed it looked kind of smudged. I picked it up and looked closer. "Guys!" I said, jumping up from my chair. "I think I have it!"

"Have what?" Daniel asked.

"Look at this!" I said, pointing to the word "out" as Daniel and Sarah walked over. "There's a box around the letter O, and there's a triangle on top of the T."

"The key is in the note!" Sarah said excitedly. She grabbed a pen and filled in the letters O and T on her paper. "What else?"

I scanned more of the note. "The star is C, the circle is N, the parentheses are H, the arrow is an O, and the smiley face is also an O." Rebecca wasn't one to turn letters into smiley faces or to doodle like Sarah did, so to see a tiny smiley face inside of the letter O made me chuckle. "The crescent is an R, the flower is an A, the lightning bolt is an M." I paused, looking for more shapes. "That's weird. The not symbol is all by itself."

"North Potomac."

"But that's only twelve letters, and there's thirteen symbols," I argued.

Sarah shook her head. "You said the not symbol was all by itself. That means it's a space, which gives us thirteen symbols." She showed me the filled in key: NOR_H _ OTOMAC.

"Wow," I said, doing a face-palm. "So, her location is exactly where her tracker shows."

around until we think we've seen what we need to see, or until someone thinks we're suspicious. Then I'll buy my suit."

"I hope you have the money for one of those suits. JX suits are pricey," Daniel said, a smirk spreading across his face.

"Wow, that's a lot bigger than it looked online," I said as we pulled into the JX parking lot. The front section of the building had three stories, and the back two sections that created the Y shape had even more stories. Dark square tiling ran up the walls, and sleek gold and black finishes on the elephant-sized windows screamed high-end. "The outside just says cha-ching," I muttered, realizing how much money I would probably be spending on a suit here. *This was a bad idea for my bank account, that's for sure.* I glanced down at my outfit, noticing the jeans, t-shirt, and sports jacket look didn't match the ultra-polished look of the customers going in and out of the building. "We're going to stick out like a sore thumb."

Daniel parked the car and turned off the engine. "No kidding." He silently stepped out of the car, adjusting the cuffs of his striped button-up shirt.

I opened my door and jumped out, squaring my shoulders and lifting my chin. "We just have to own it."

Daniel smirked. "Sure."

We walked inside, and I had to force myself to keep my jaw from dropping. The walls were black, with metal pillars drawing your eye to the vaulted ceiling, which had metal beams running across it. All the clothing racks were brass, and there were huge brass light fixtures everywhere. I glanced at Daniel. "There's no way I can afford to rent a suit from here, let alone buy one," I whispered.

Before Daniel could reply, an employee walked up to us. "Welcome. Can I help you find anything?"

"Wedding suits," Daniel answered, nodding at me. "He's getting married soon, and I'm his best man."

I felt my face grow warm as the lady directed us to the left-hand side of the store. *I haven't even asked Rebecca to marry me yet,* I thought, wishing Daniel had said business suits.

"If you need a break between browsing and getting fitted for your suit, there is a coffee shop out in the courtyard," the lady said, motioning to the double doors on the back wall.

"Thank you," I said, my stomach dropping at the price tags surrounding me. *Coffee might be the only thing I can afford here.*

As we thumbed through the suits, Daniel whispered, "What's the plan, Romeo?"

I rolled my eyes. "To somehow avoid buying a suit," I replied, glancing at the two-thousand-dollar price tag on the tuxedo in my hand. "And get a coffee in the courtyard. I think that's the direction we need to head if we want to look around."

Daniel nodded. Sarah spoke up in our earpieces, "You might want to wait a while before going to get the coffee. Otherwise you won't seem very serious about getting a suit."

"Copy that," I replied, feeling impatient to do sleuthing instead of looking at suits I couldn't afford to buy.

I continued looking at suit and tuxedo styles, asking silly questions of the salesmen who would come to offer their assistance and opinions on what I would look best in, all the while inwardly banging my head against an imaginary wall. I didn't want a two-thousand-dollar tuxedo. I wanted to find Rebecca.

Once Sarah gave the go-ahead, Daniel and I went to the courtyard. We walked toward the coffee shop. I glanced around, noticing how large this courtyard was. Metal tables and chairs dotted the open area. A large, square, concrete pot filled with flowers and a few palm trees underneath a glass ceiling was the focal point of the courtyard. The coffee shop was to the left of the courtyard. To the right was a small sandwich shop. The far wall had two sets of double-doors, both with scanners next to them. *Rebecca must be through those doors somewhere.* "How far away is Rebecca's tracker from our location?" I asked Sarah.

"Well, the tracker has been moving around some, but she's about thirty yards north of you right now," Sarah replied.

So, through those double-doors, I thought. *Man, this building is huge.*

We ordered coffee, then looked at the scanners by the doors. "Badge scanners," Daniel muttered as we walked past.

I nodded. "Looks like we may need some badges."

We decided Daniel would stay in the courtyard and try to get information about the badges for the scanners. "I'll try to get some pictures of a badge, or better yet get my hands on one so we can make some fakes," he said.

"Luke should go back to looking at the suits while you do that," Sarah said through our earpieces. "That way you'll seem less suspicious."

"I'd prefer to help with the badges," I replied, sighing.

Daniel shrugged. "Sarah's right. Plus, if that big dude who was with Rebecca the other day shows up, he might recognize you. It's probably best for you to go get fitted for a suit." He finished his statement with a wink.

I frowned and rolled my eyes. "I guess I'll go drain my bank account while you have fun scouting."

I spent the next hour getting fitted for a suit and trying to decide what color Rebecca would want me to pick. I went with a traditional black suit, knowing Rebecca wasn't one for frills or bright colors. *This is weird to pick out a suit when I haven't even asked her to marry me yet,* I thought nervously. I tried not to groan as I paid for the suit and the alterations the salesman insisted needed made. I walked to the front door and notified Daniel that I had purchased the suit and was leaving.

"I'll meet you at the car," he replied.

I walked out to the car and jumped in the driver's seat. *I wonder if that was the right suit to choose,* I thought, butterflies in my stomach. I didn't know why I felt so nervous about buying this suit. My usual confidence was replaced with terror. *What if she says no?* I cringed. *Why would I think that? I bought the ring... I was quite sure she would say yes. Why is this mission making me doubt everything?*

Daniel opened the car door and jumped into the passenger seat. "Let's go."

"Got what you needed?" I asked, starting the engine.

"I think so. I grabbed a badge on the janitor's cart while he was away. I got pictures and measurements and sent them to Sarah. Just barely got the badge back on his cart in time before he came back." Daniel chuckled. "I'm glad you took so long on that suit. It was a while before I could get ahold of a badge."

I grinned, trying not to think anymore about the money I'd spent. "Well, let's get some fake badges made and sneak in!"

"Wow, this place is nice," Sarah said as we walked up to the JX store.

Daniel opened the door and we hurried inside. The place was much busier than two days earlier. We looked up the store hours and which times were the busiest. We wanted to be able to slip through the store into the courtyard without much notice. Friday afternoon looked like the best time.

We quickly made our way to the courtyard. There was a decent coffee line and several of the tables were full. I noticed more employees going in and out the doors with the scanners. Most of the employees dressed business casual, so we dressed the part. We all wore dress pants, Daniel and I wore button-up shirts, and Sarah wore a nice blouse.

"So far so good," Daniel said as we walked up to the doors unnoticed. He pulled his fake badge from his pocket. We printed fake badges that mimicked the one the janitor had, with photos, barcodes, employee information, and watermarking. The badges looked pretty convincing. The only problem was they all had the same barcode as the janitor. *I hope this works*, I thought, praying it would.

Daniel placed his badge on the glass scanner. The light above the scanner flashed green and we heard the door unbolt. I let out a breath and pushed the door open. We all walked in, and I silently prayed that no one would notice we walked in as a group instead of individually.

We walked down a short hallway to another courtyard. My eyes widened at the mass of people milling about. There was obviously more going on back here than JX clothing work. We made our way through the crowd. I could tell from the snippets of conversation floating past that there was some sort of conference happening. We slowed our pace and stopped at one of the tables in the middle of the room. I glanced around. Another coffee shop was on the left of the courtyard, and several offices with glass windows lined the courtyard. Like the other courtyard, metal tables dotted the room, but the center had office-style leather chairs with foldout desks on the right armrest. On the far end, two hallways split off in a Y shape.

"Looks like most people are headed down the hall on the left," Daniel said quietly.

I nodded toward the door on the right. "I overheard some people talking about a conference, and they're headed right."

"Which way should we go?" Sarah asked. "Should we stay with the large crowd, so we don't stand out?"

I thought for a minute. "Probably." I paused as a group of employees bumped into our table. "How far are we from Rebecca's tracker?"

Sarah tapped on her watch. "We're practically on top of her. She must be going with one of these two groups."

"But you can't tell which?" Daniel asked.

Sarah shook her head. "It's a guessing game at this point."

If Rebecca is working at the top, then she's got to be going with the smaller crowd, I thought, watching people walk past. I pondered for a moment if I should go with my gut feeling. *They seem to be keeping close tabs on her, and that would be challenging in the larger crowd.* "Let's go right."

Sarah nodded. "That's what I was thinking."

I led the way down the hall, going slow so we could stay behind most of the crowd. As I watched people scurry down the hall, I estimated there were about forty people headed this way. *I hope we can still blend in.*

"I think you're headed the wrong way."

I tensed and stepped back as a man blocked my path. He was wearing a dark suit and sunglasses, and he had a badge pinned to his lapel. "Excuse me?" I asked, hoping my tone sounded innocent.

The man pointed back the way we came. "You're supposed to be going down the hall on the left. This way's for executives only."

"Oh," I said, faking a laugh. "We're new here, and I struggle with directions. I was sure this was the right way."

Sarah placed her hands on her hips. "I told you we were headed the wrong way."

"Sorry about that," Daniel said, taking a step back. "We'll get going."

We headed down the hall a few paces before the guard caught back up with us. "Hold on a minute. When did you start working here?"

I glanced at Sarah and Daniel, not sure what would sound the most convincing. Daniel slid his fingers into the number three. "Three weeks ago," I replied confidently.

The guard hesitated. "Let me see some ID."

We pulled out our badges and I silently prayed he wouldn't inspect them too long.

After quickly glancing at our badges, he nodded and muttered, "Have a nice day," then headed back down the hall.

I sighed with relief and stuck my badge back in my pocket. "That was close."

"Now what?" Daniel asked. "Do we go to the other meeting instead of this one?"

Sarah sighed. "I think we have to. He said this way was for executive's only, and he could tell we didn't belong."

I nodded, my stomach sinking a little. "Let's try the other meeting and see if we can learn anything there." *Less chance of seeing Rebecca there, though.*

We hurried back to the courtyard that was now mostly empty and went down the left hall. There was a bottleneck at the end of the hall.

"I wonder what's taking so long," Daniel muttered as we waited for the crowd to move.

Daniel and Sarah continued talking, but my mind wandered back to Rebecca. *Lord, keep her safe,* I prayed for what felt like the millionth time. I didn't like being on this mission without her, and more than that I didn't like that she was in a dangerous position on this mission. I never liked it when my friends were in dangerous positions, but I could usually keep my cool about it. It was different with Rebecca, though. I just wanted to be by her side, to know that if she were in danger, at least I'd be there to fight with her. I shook my head and looked back at the crowd, trying to focus on the mission at hand.

The crowd had moved forward a few yards. I moved over by the wall to try and see the door. I noticed the door opening and closing slightly, I assumed to let only one person in at a time. *That's weird. This is a big group to only let them in one at a time.* The time ticked by slowly as we moved one step forward every minute. *It'll be New Year's by the time we reach the door,* I thought, yawning. I noticed many others in the crowd had gotten their phones out, and no one acted like this was out of place. *Do they check every badge?*

The crowd began to move into more of a line, and I could see along the wall to the door. At the door to the conference room stood two guards. In between them was a security camera. I watched as someone walked up to the scanner, put their face down by it, and then the door opened. My jaw dropped. "Guys, they have a retinal scanner."

Daniel moved over by me. "Seriously?"

We watched as another person looked at the scanner and was allowed in. I glanced over at Daniel. "We can't fool that."

"We're not getting into that conference," Sarah said, shaking her head. "We need to get out of here before anyone notices."

I nodded. "Let's go."

As we wove back down the hall to the courtyard, I kept my eyes open for sign of the security guard who'd stopped us earlier. The courtyard was almost deserted. We hurried through the short hall, back through the JX courtyard and clothing store, and out the front doors.

"Well that was helpful," Daniel said sarcastically.

No kidding, I thought. *We just sneaked inside for nothing.* "Let's come up with a plan B."

CHAPTER 6

Why do I wake up early when there's nothing to do? I wondered, plopping down on the couch. It was not even five yet, but my brain was wide awake. *We're still stuck, and waking up early isn't going to help anything.* I sighed and prayed, *Lord, please help us find a lead.*

I got up and looked out the window at the dark sky, a soft hue at the horizon signaling the coming sunrise. I stared at the city lights, wishing there were less of them so that the stars would be more visible. Stars always reminded me of how big God was and yet He still cared about my life.

I jumped at a light tap on the door. I glanced at the clock on the wall. *4:55. Who would be here this early?* I thought, wondering if it was my imagination. I heard another tap on the door. *That's not my imagination.* I tip-toed to the door and slowly opened it. No one was there. I glanced down the dark hall and saw someone opening the stairwell door. I jogged down the hall and pushed the stairwell door open. Someone was running down the stairs. Someone with long, dark hair. *Rebecca?* I hurried down the stairs after her, hoping my mind wasn't playing tricks on me.

I heard the door open and close to the outside, and that's when I realized I didn't have my room key with me. *If I follow her outside, I won't be able to get back in.* I hurried to the door and pushed it open, using my foot to keep it open. "Rebecca?" I called to the form that was vanishing into the darkness.

She stopped moving and turned around. "You didn't see me, okay?" she replied. I expected her to dash away, but she kept standing there. "Okay?"

"Yeah, sure," I replied, swallowing the tightness in my throat. I wanted to run and give her a hug, or keep talking, or something, but I wasn't sure if she was alone. I didn't want to jeopardize anything. I felt like I needed to say something, anything, before she left. As she took a step back, I blurted, "I love you." My face felt like it burst into flames, and I hoped she couldn't tell with the dim lighting around the building. "I'm praying for you. Don't get yourself hurt, okay?"

"Thanks. And same to you." I couldn't see her face, but I could hear the smile in her voice. "Check your door." With that she jogged away.

I couldn't keep the smile from my face as I walked back up the stairs. *Same to you? I hope that was for the 'I love you' and not just the 'don't get hurt' part.* Knowing Rebecca, I assumed the 'same' referred to everything. I hurried back to the room door and found a sticky note by the handle. There were three names on the note. I pulled the note off the handle and then grimaced as I knocked on the door. *I hope someone heard that,* I thought, wishing I had grabbed my room key or my phone. I knocked again. *This might be a while.* I sat down and leaned against the door.

I stared at the door across the hall, my mind going back to Rebecca, wondering why she left the note without talking to any of us. The tension between wanting to keep my girlfriend safe and needing to stay on task for the mission was becoming frustrating. *Is it even worth it?* The thought popped into my head unexpectedly. *To keep sticking with this mission if it means Rebecca isn't safe?* I shook my head. *This isn't just about Rebecca. But how do I balance this mission with keeping her safe? Can I, even?*

An hour later, Daniel opened the door, and I fell backward. "What are you doing out here?" he whispered.

I stood up and stretched. "We've got a note."

Daniel looked confused as he let me in. "A note?"

"Rebecca left this on our door." I handed him the sticky note.

"Three names. That's it?"

I nodded. "I think we need to do some research."

We spent the day researching the three names Rebecca gave us. One was Cody Carter, who turned out to be the big guy I'd run into the other day. He worked as a security officer at JX. The next was Amy Landon, a social media director for a presidential candidate, Jeorge Filips. The third person was Austin Banks, a local news anchor.

"What an odd bunch of people," Sarah said, looking over the info we'd gathered. "What do they even have in common?"

"The sticky note," I joked.

Sarah smirked but Daniel ignored my comment. "I think that's our next move. Find out what these three really have in common. I mean, a political social media director and a local news anchor are sort of related, but where does the JX security guard fit in?"

"Well, if JX is a front for MAX, maybe he's got people on the inside of the media so that when he makes his move, he'll get media coverage," I suggested.

Sarah nodded. "That's very likely."

"So, what's the plan?" I crossed my arms.

Daniel tapped his chin. "Well, Rebecca gave us three names and there's three of us. We each trail someone and try to gather info."

"That leaves us with no back-up if something goes wrong," Sarah replied nervously.

I nodded. "But that might be a risk we have to take. I think Sarah can trail Amy, I'll take Austin, and Daniel, you can take Cody. That way Cody won't recognize me."

Daniel nodded. "And we can all stay in constant communication and be ready to back each other up if necessary. We can also let Truth Squad know the plan so that if something happens where we can't help each other, we'll have someone on standby."

Sarah nodded, but she didn't look any less nervous about the plan. I cracked a smile, trying to suppress my own nervousness about this plan. "Let's pray instead of worrying."

We bowed our heads and Daniel offered a quick prayer. "Lord, thank You for giving us a new lead. We have a plan, but it seems a little risky. Please give us wisdom and protection as we investigate MAX, and help us to get to the bottom of what's going on."

And keep Rebecca safe, too, I added silently. "Amen."

"Can I help you?"

I cringed inwardly but put on a bright smile as I faced the lady at the front desk. I had hoped to sneak into the local news station without being spotted, but the front door seemed to be my only way in, and there were not a whole lot of people coming in to see the local news. "Hi, I was wondering where I could go to apply for an internship?" Today, I was playing up the fact that I looked like a high schooler instead of an adult.

I wore jeans and a zip-up hoodie, and I swooped the front of my hair back with a little more drama than normal so that I looked more in style.

The lady gave me a sympathetic smile. "We do all our internship applications online."

"Oh." I let my shoulders fall as I looked around the room. I hoped if I acted dejected enough, she would offer to let me sit in on the broadcasting. High schoolers interested in broadcasting often did that sort of thing.

Luckily, my routine worked. The lady glanced at the clock and then told me that they would be broadcasting in a few minutes. "Would you like to sit in and watch? Afterward, I'm sure Austin would be willing to answer a few questions."

I smiled. "That would be cool. Thanks!"

For the next hour, I sat on a metal folding chair in the corner of the broadcasting room. Austin was on the shorter end with a perfectly tanned complexion, and dark hair and eyes. He had the typical news-caster voice, deep and commanding. He covered local incidents as well as a few national events. During his local announcements, Austin mentioned that a development block had been purchased by JX. I pulled out my phone and made a note of the development block to look up later.

After the film crew called cut, Austin talked to his producer for a minute, then came up and shook my hand. "Well, young man, what did you think of the broadcast?"

I grinned, finding it hilarious to be called "young man" by a guy only five years older than me. "Great! There's so much more going on behind the scenes with the camera crew and stuff than I expected," I replied.

Austin nodded. "What's your name?"

"Tim Jonson."

He asked questions about my interest in broadcasting, and I gave him my rehearsed answers. I was interested in the film side of things because I didn't have the voice for broadcasting. I had done a little bit of research ahead of time so that I could sound genuinely interested in broadcasting, and it paid off. "What do you think about job shadowing the crew for the next couple days? We can't do a full internship because we're pretty busy right now, but a few days of job shadowing should be good enough to know if this is a career you want to pursue."

I nodded, mentally noting his comments about being busy. The place seemed rather deserted for being super busy. *Is he busy with MAX stuff?* I wondered hopefully.

That evening back at the hotel, we went over what we'd accomplished while eating turkey sandwiches and maple bars. I was the one who bought dinner, which of course meant doughnuts for dessert was mandatory. "I'll be job shadowing the news crew for the next two days," I said after telling Daniel and Sarah about the development property JX had bought. After I left the news station, I'd looked up the location JX had bought. It was ten acres of land behind the JX headquarters. There were already a few warehouses on the property.

"Do you think I'd be able to check out the warehouses?" Daniel asked. "I won't be able to follow Cody tomorrow, anyways. He took a flight to Denver and, from what I overheard, he won't be back for a few days."

I shrugged. "It's worth a shot."

Sarah yawned. "I didn't learn much today. Amy filmed a video in front of the capitol building this morning, but other than that, she spent most of the day working in a coffee shop by herself."

"So, I guess we'll keep investigating what we can while you go undercover with the news team," Daniel said. "Hopefully something useful turns up."

I grinned. "And until then, we have plenty of time to enjoy these maple bars." I picked mine up and took a huge bite. "Mmm!" I said, savoring the sweet, sticky dessert. "I could get used to this."

Daniel laughed and rolled his eyes. "I think you already are."

Eight a.m. sharp I was back at the news station, learning the ropes of camera work. From nine till eleven, I helped with cueing Austin when to start and stop for commercial breaks. I actually found it fun to work with the crew and see all the camera men and sound techs orchestrate things. But two hours of talking about local news left me with no leads on MAX.

After Austin's segment ended, it was the lunch break. "After lunch you can join the crew as we cover the feel-good story for the afternoon," Austin said as we walked to the lunchroom.

"What's the feel-good story for today?" I asked.

"Local high-schooler hosts bake-off for a charity fundraiser," Austin said as though reading a headline. He grabbed a sack lunch from the office fridge and sat at one of the plastic tables. I grabbed my own lunch and joined him. "I think you'll enjoy this afternoon. The camera crew does more to set up the right shot when we're out 'in the field,' as we like to say," Austin explained.

"Sounds cool!" I replied before biting into my sandwich.

After lunch, we loaded up the film equipment and headed to the high school. The crew spent a couple hours filming interviews and even a snippet of the bake-off. With a final interview explaining how viewers at home could donate to the charity organization, the crew packed the film equipment back up. *Still no information about MAX,* I thought, climbing into the van for the ride home. *Almost a full day under-cover, and I've learned nothing.*

"Before you go, Tim, you'll need to fill out a form saying how many hours you shadowed today," Austin said when we got back to the studio. I nodded and followed him to his office. Austin got out a form from a file cabinet and handed it to me when his phone rang. He pulled it from his pocket and glanced at the screen. "I'll need to take this. Just fill out the form and leave it on my desk when you finish."

I nodded and began filling out the form, listening for which direction Austin's footsteps would head as he left. He went right. I hurried to the door and saw the door to the room beside Austin's office finish closing. I glanced around Austin's office. There was a vent at the top of the wall connecting the two rooms. Pushing Austin's rolling chair over to the wall, I jumped up and put my ear up by the vent. I could barely hear Austin's voice in the other room. I took off my watch and turned on the record function, then set it to amplify distant sounds. I also turned on the voice-to-text feature so I could see what was being recorded.

Austin's words started scrolling across my watch. "So, what time does the press need to be there?" Pause. "Okay, yeah, we can be there then." Pause. "Is there anything you want us to say or to ask? Mmm-hmm." There was a long pause this time. I wished he were talking on speakerphone so I could know what the other end of the line was saying. I waited, expecting some sort of clue for Austin's next comment, but instead he said, "I'd better get going." I stopped the recording on my watch and lightly jumped down from the chair, pushing it back into place. I hurriedly filled out the time and signed my alias to Austin's form and then left the office, praying not to run into Austin as I left.

"Any luck today?" I asked Daniel and Sarah as they walked into the hotel room. I'd beat them back since my time shadowing the news crew ended at four. Neither looked excited, but they didn't look down either, so I hoped for the best.

"Sort of," Sarah replied, setting down her purse on the counter. She grabbed a glass from the kitchenette cabinet and filled it with water. "Amy spent the morning at a coffee shop editing the video she filmed at the capitol. It looked like a campaign ad from what I could see, but of course I couldn't hear the audio."

"Sarah joined me at the warehouses after lunch," Daniel said, sitting down at the table opposite me.

"Some friends met Amy for lunch," Sarah explained, "and afterward they went to the mall. It didn't take long to realize there was nothing to the trip except a few friends hanging out."

"So, basically you learned that Amy is making a campaign ad, which isn't surprising since she's the social media manager for a political candidate," I summarized.

Sarah nodded, and Daniel continued his side of the story. "There was a lot going on at the new property JX bought. People were coming and going like an ant colony. Several of the warehouses were taken down, some tents were set up, there was a stage put in, and temporary metal fencing was put up around the stage and around the property."

I tilted my head thoughtfully. "Sounds like they're setting up for a concert. Which I am totally down for." I slapped the table excitedly. "Do you remember that one concert we went to—"

"Luke, you're getting distracted," Sarah said, joining us at the table.

I grinned to hide my disappointment over not finishing my reminiscence. "My specialty. Anyhow, there's a stage and tents and fencing. Continue." I swung my arm grandly toward Daniel.

"This was about the time Sarah showed up. We decided to sneak onto the property during the lunch break through the back. All of the work was at the front half of the property by the road. We peeked inside the warehouses that we could, but most were empty until we got closer to the construction site."

Sarah nodded. "Then we found warehouses full of lighting equipment, construction equipment, a lot of extension cords, and we also found boxes of flyers for a political candidate."

I noticed Sarah's eyes lit up, so I jumped in with a guess. "Jeorge Filips, the one Amy works for?" Sarah nodded. "So, wait, does that mean this set-up is for a political rally?"

Daniel nodded. "That's what we're thinking."

"Hmm." I crossed my arms, thinking back to Austin's phone call. "I overheard Austin on the phone today talking about a time to be somewhere and specific questions to ask. While it could be for any news interview, I wonder if he could be going to the rally." Daniel raised an eyebrow skeptically, so I added, "It's a stretch since I didn't hear the whole phone conversation. But I'm thinking that these three clues are hinting that MAX is involved with politics somehow."

"Why, though?" Sarah asked, resting her chin in her hands. She tilted her head to the side as she thought. *Exactly like Rebecca does,* I thought wistfully.

"Up till this point, MAX has been connected to power plants. Why the change to politics?" she asked.

Daniel shook his head. "There has to be some sort of connection." He sighed. "We've got all these random pieces of info, but we're not any closer to knowing who's behind MAX."

Sarah frowned and rubbed her forehead. "The election is in five weeks. If MAX is trying to do something related to the election, then we've got to figure this out fast."

I nodded, frowning. "I wish we could talk to Rebecca. This would be so much easier if we had more of her info."

Sarah shook her head. "We can't risk that." We sat in silence for a moment. "So, what next?"

Daniel glanced at his watch. "I'd say dinner is next."

"Good, because I'm starving!" I exclaimed, trying to lighten the mood.

Daniel grinned. "Let's eat dinner and get a good night's rest. And tomorrow we'll continue our undercover work."

The next morning, I was back with the film crew for my second and last day of shadowing. *Lord, please help me, and Daniel and Sarah, too, to find some kind of lead,* I prayed as I walked to the studio.

The day of filming was almost identical to the day before. Austin had his morning segment, then in the afternoon we went on the street, this time for people's thoughts about a new shopping center being put in. While hearing people's differing opinions about the shopping center was interesting, I was frustrated to find no leads about MAX. As we rode in the van back to the studio, one of the cameramen, Sam, elbowed me and said, "Why do you look so gloomy?"

I blinked, not realizing I had let my disappointment show. "Oh, nothing much. Just realizing I'm almost done shadowing you guys." I smiled. "It's been fun."

Sam smiled, revealing a missing tooth. "I'm glad you've enjoyed yourself, kid."

A younger cameraman in the row behind us clasped Sam's shoulder. "I know! We're covering the rally tomorrow. He should come with us."

Sam's face brightened. "That's right! A rally's a great learning experience, kid." He slapped my shoulder and I grinned to hide my grimace.

"That would be cool!" I said.

Austin turned around in the passenger seat, his eyes flaming. I couldn't tell if he was angry or worried. "What?"

Sam jumped in. "Austin, we should take the kid with us to the rally. It'll be a great learning experience, especially since he's seriously interested in broadcasting and filming." Sam made a face at Austin, and I got the feeling that Sam pulled more weight at the studio than Austin.

Austin sighed and turned to face the road. "Fine. So long as he doesn't get in my way."

I grinned. "Sweet!"

Sam filled me in on the details of when and where for the rally, what I needed to wear, what credentials I needed to get in as a part of the camera crew. "Just show up early and we'll have the pass you need."

I was glad I was faking being a high-school student, because I couldn't have hidden my excitement if I wanted to. "Thanks for letting me shadow you for one more day, Sam. I really appreciate it," I said as I left the studio that day.

"No problem, kid."

I hurried back to the hotel room, excited to see Daniel and Sarah were already back from their undercover work.

"Guess what?" I yelled as I ran into the room.

"Okay, that was a little loud," Sarah said, covering her ears. She sat in front of the computer and didn't even look up.

"Sorry," I said, smiling apologetically. I lowered my voice and tried again. "Guess what?"

"You must've learned something good," Daniel said. "Which is a good thing for us, because we didn't learn anything today."

"We've got a lead!" I said excitedly.

Sarah popped her head up from the computer. "We do?"

I nodded. "I'm taking this broadcasting gig to the political rally tomorrow. One of the camera crewmen suggested I tag along for more experience. Austin was not happy about that, but since the whole crew thought it would be a good experience, he agreed for me to tag along."

Daniel gave me a high-five. "That's the best news yet."

"If Austin wasn't happy about you going, do you think MAX might be there?" Sarah asked.

I nodded and grinned. "That's what I'm hoping for."

CHAPTER 7

"Tim!"

I stuck my keys in my pocket and waved back at Sam who was standing on the sidewalk waving his arm in huge circles. Sam was obviously energized for the rally. I was too. "How's it going?" I said, reaching Sam and shaking his hand. I had just dropped Daniel off a block behind the JX warehouses. Daniel was going to pose as a janitor, using the badge we'd copied from before. Sarah stayed back at the hotel to monitor communications and security camera footage.

"Here's your badge," Sam said, taking one of the three lanyards off from around his neck and handing it to me. "I'm still waiting for Jay to show up."

I looked down at my official press badge, feeling a wave of excitement. I was going undercover as a part of the press to a political rally. Totally new for me. "So, how is the day going to go?" I asked.

Sam grinned. "You nervous, kid?" I just shrugged. "It's pretty simple. We film people at the rally, interview your average voter as well as more prominent individuals, and see if we can get in some questions during the press conference. I think there may be a speech happening, so we'll film that, too." Sam rolled his shoulders. "It'll be a long day, trust me. So, don't use up all that energy in the first hour being nervous."

I laughed. "I'll try to remember that."

Daniel came in over my coms. "I'm in."

I felt relief inwardly, but kept a straight face while Sarah replied and took notes on Daniel's whereabouts. Being undercover with the press would be harder on my end since I probably wouldn't have very many opportunities to communicate directly to Daniel and Sarah.

After Jay showed up, we entered the rally grounds through a special entrance just for the media. We set up movable cameras, and I was put on the sound mic. Austin was a few minutes late. "What took you so long?" Sam asked, jokingly punching Austin's shoulder.

Austin rolled his eyes. "Just trying to keep up with what the other news outlets are doing. Let's get to work."

The crew interviewed several people as they waited in line for the rally. Some prominent individuals were interviewed, like the mayor and a couple celebrities who were endorsing different candidates. Through the course of the interviews, I noticed that this rally was for several Congressional and Senate candidates from along the east coast, more than I had originally thought would be there. *This will make learning about MAX more difficult,* I thought. I couldn't help but wonder what would happen if we failed at stopping MAX and he gained some kind of access to national government. *What would that mean for our country? For Truth Squad? For Christians, even? If this MAX guy is someone like Zaiden...* I shuddered at the thought of what life might be like under that kind of control.

After filming a segment of Austin describing the atmosphere of the rally, we cut the filming and joined the rest of the press for the press conference. I was stopped at the door.

"I'm sorry, but interns are not allowed at this press debriefing." The security officer smiled kindly as I stepped aside, and she continued checking people's badges.

Sam shrugged. "Well, sorry kid. Rules are rules. I guess you'll have to wait around for a while."

"Can I get some snacks at the concession stand while I wait?" I asked.

Sam nodded. "Stay close by, though. We'll need to get back to filming quickly after the press conference is over."

After Sam went inside, I made my way toward the concession stand. "I've got a break," I muttered into my coms. "What's up?"

"Daniel is about twenty yards east of you," Sarah directed.

I looked at my watch's compass to find east, then walked that direction. I found Daniel changing the trash bag in one of the recycling bins. "It's amazing how quickly these have filled up when the rally hasn't even officially started."

I smirked. Daniel was really getting into character. "How's the sleuthing going?"

Daniel shrugged. "I haven't learned much. When I first got here, I saw Austin talking to a group of security officers for a while before joining you. I tried to follow them, but they went into an authorized-personnel-only area."

"So, Austin was not late because of talking to other press. Interesting."

"I've been keeping my ears open for any word about MAX or powerplants or something, but I haven't heard anything," Daniel said, locking the recycling lid back into place.

I crossed my arms. "So, if we want to learn anything, we need into the authorized-personnel-only area."

"An interning press badge isn't going to cut it," Daniel replied, pushing his gray and yellow cart toward the next recycling bin.

I stopped walking and looked around, thinking. *Daniel was able to sneak in through the back unnoticed.* Everywhere I looked there were tents and movable fences. There were so many people milling about, it would be easy to cross a barrier with the right distractions. *We just need to find a way in besides the door Daniel saw,* I thought.

I caught back up to Daniel and told him my idea. "Sounds good," he said. Daniel left his cart by the recycling bin and led the way to the tent.

The authorized-personnel-only tent was on the left side of the ginormous stage. An audience was slowly filling the arena, but to get to the tent you had to walk down a long, gated walkway that had two security checkpoints. Looking around, I noticed the tents on each side of the stage were wedged between the stage and a warehouse. *So, they're using the warehouses to keep people from sneaking around the sides,* I thought. "Where did you sneak in?" I asked Daniel.

He pointed to the other side of the stage. "I just followed the fence around the property until I got to the temporary fencing here. No one was around, so I just hopped over and went searching for janitor supplies."

"So, if there's space on the sides of the warehouses, we can go around this side and try to find a way into the tent from the back," I said quietly. Daniel nodded and we made our way to the temporary fencing. Daniel nodded toward a guard who was keeping an eye on us, so we leaned against the rail and chatted about nothing, waiting for the guard to stop watching us. Eventually, a lady came up to the guard, her high pitch voice and frantic hand motions starting a small commotion around her. The guard turned his back to us. Daniel hopped over the fence, and I followed. We hurried to the warehouse and stood in the shadows for a second, listening for any sign of having been spotted.

"I think we're clear," Daniel said. I nodded and we sprinted down the path between the warehouse and fence. I kept my eyes open for security cameras, but I didn't see anything suspicious.

We stopped at the edge of the warehouse, and Daniel peeked around the corner. A flash of red caught my eye. I turned to scan my surroundings. A red bird with black wings was resting on the fence next to me. *Never mind, not a danger,* I thought, smiling as the bird cocked its head back and forth as though sizing me up.

"Go!" Daniel took off running.

I shook my head, jolted back to the mission. *I totally missed what's going on.* I quickly glanced around the warehouse corner and, praying that no one would spot us, took off after Daniel.

Daniel made a face as I joined him behind a tent wall. "That was a delayed reaction," he muttered.

I grinnèd sheepishly. "Sorry, I was distracted."

Daniel just rolled his eyes. "Let's skirt the tent and see if we can find a way in. Watch out for the plastic windows, though."

I followed Daniel around the tent, ducking whenever we passed a window. There was a lot of noise coming from inside the tent. I could hear fans running, footsteps moving past the tent wall, and a cacophony of muddled conversations drifting through the wall.

Daniel paused when we reached the tent edge. Groups of people milled around behind the tent. "We can't sneak out this way. We'll be too conspicuous."

"So, now what?" I looked around, trying to think up a new plan. Suddenly, a whistle blew.

"Move back," Daniel said, backing away from the tent corner.

I hurried back a few yards. "What's going on?"

"Everyone is headed inside this tent," Daniel said, tapping the white tarp beside us.

I raised an eyebrow. "Everyone? Does that mean we could slip in?"

Daniel shrugged. "Possibly."

I pulled out my phone and stuck the camera up by the nearest plastic window. After recording video for a few seconds, I hurried back to Daniel and watched the footage. The tent looked packed, like some kind of meeting was happening. "Maybe we don't need to sneak in, we can just stick a recording device under the tent wall."

Daniel shook his head. "We can't guarantee that will pick up the sound."

"So, we're just gonna go for it?" Daniel nodded. I grinned. "Let's do this." I jumped up and rounded the corner of the tent.

"How's it going? What's going on?" Sarah asked through our coms.

"We're infiltrating the authorized-personnel-only area," Daniel replied.

I stopped walking and glanced around. While most people were headed into the giant white tent, a smaller tent labeled "Security, Makeup, Staging" had a group of people headed inside it as well. I glanced at Daniel and nodded toward the smaller tent. Daniel gave me a thumbs up. I pulled my shoulders back and walked confidently in the direction of the tent, hoping I looked like I belonged there.

A guard was at the tent entrance, checking badges. I pulled out my press badge and flashed it quickly, my heartbeat accelerating. *Please let us in.* The guard just nodded without paying me much attention, and I hurried inside, hoping Daniel was behind me.

I continued forward, following the group in front of me and acting like I knew what I was doing. "You still with me, Daniel?" I muttered into my coms.

"Yeah, just a couple people behind you."

Everyone came to a halt toward the back of the tent. Like the sign on the door indicated, there was a row of professionally dressed men and women getting their makeup and hair done. In the very back of the tent were several large computer screens showing footage from around the rally site. To my left was a metal storage unit with boxes labeled "microphones," "mic stands," "podium," and so on.

Daniel nudged me. "What's going on in here?" he muttered.

I shrugged. "Just people getting ready for the rally, I guess. Maybe we can find out who MAX is if we stay around."

"Hey!" I turned to the commanding voice, seeing a short man with round glasses, a bright red tie, and an angry face almost the same color as his tie. "Don't just stand there. We're running behind schedule. Get these boxes moved. Let's go!"

I nodded and Daniel and I each picked up a box. No one else grabbed any boxes, and I began to feel nervous. After leaving the tent, I glanced at Daniel. "Where exactly do we take these?"

"I would assume to the stage. Let's just hope that's where they go, otherwise people will know we don't belong here."

"Hey, pick up the pace, will you? We're running behind and don't have time for your lollygagging."

My heart skipped a beat hearing the familiar voice. I turned and saw Rebecca coming up behind us, also carrying a box. "Yes, ma'am."

"We're headed to the backstage of the stage, in case your brains have left you," she said in a sarcastic tone, but she smiled as she walked past us.

Daniel and I fell in step behind her. She led us to a small, curtained-off area behind the stage. There were stacks of boxes already lining the room. "Leave the boxes here." She set down her box and lowered her voice. "Once you've moved all the boxes, meet me at the white trailer on the west side." With that, she spun on her heel and left.

I raised an eyebrow at Daniel, and he shrugged. "I guess that's the plan, then."

We hurried back to the makeup and staging room and continued moving boxes. Just as we finished the last load and were leaving the backstage room, the man with the red tie called us on stage to help set up the sound system.

I sighed. "Really?"

"We'll have to wait on meeting with Rebecca," Daniel said, leading the way up the steps to the stage.

We spent the next thirty minutes helping with the stage set-up. Finally, the man with the red tie was called to meet with someone, and Daniel and I headed for the white trailer Rebecca had indicated. The trailer was at the farthest corner of the fenced-in area.

Sarah jumped in on our coms. "Guys, I can't find the security cameras in your area."

"Okay, we'll keep our eyes open for any tails," Daniel replied as we reached the trailer.

It was a typical camping trailer instead of one of the fancy production trailers the rest of the park was filled with. No one was around, and I couldn't see any lights from the trailer windows. I pulled on the door handle, and it swung open.

Daniel stepped inside and I followed. "Rebecca?" he whispered. We waited, but no one replied.

"Let's just look around," I said, noting how empty the trailer was. "I'll check the kitchen cabinets." Daniel nodded and headed to the back half of the trailer where the bed was. I opened the top cupboards. They were empty. I noticed water slowly dripping from the sink, so I assumed someone had been there recently. I rubbed my finger across the laminate counter, noticing it was slightly damp. *So, someone washed the counter recently,* I thought, opening the bottom cabinet doors. The shelves were empty, but there was an envelope taped to the underside of the counter. I pulled the envelope out and opened it. Inside were two badges, one with my picture and one with Daniel's. There was also a piece of paper with Rebecca's handwriting, looking rushed. "You'll find your uniforms under the bed. You're stationed at the north-east corner of the stage. Don't forget the sunglasses." She'd drawn a smiley face next to her note, and a huge smile spread across my face.

"Look under the bed," I called to Daniel.

Daniel walked out of the room holding a clear bag labeled security. "Already did."

I showed Daniel Rebecca's note and then we quickly put on our new uniforms over our clothes. We checked out the windows for anyone headed our way. The coast was clear, so we hurried back outside. "To the north-east corner of the stage we go," I said.

Daniel nodded. "We'd better hurry. The rally could start any minute."

We reached our post just as the first speaker stepped onto the stage. Two other guards were already there.

"You're late," the taller man said. He stepped away from his post.

"My apologies," I replied, taking his place. "Anything of note?"

Both guards shook their heads and then walked away. I looked across the stage at the other two guards and mimicked their stances, standing straight with my arms behind my back. Daniel did the same.

"What exactly does Rebecca expect us to learn here?" Daniel muttered as the speaker droned on about politics.

"I'm not sure." I glanced around. There was media everywhere. The crowd was full of people sporting different political candidate gear.

"Look to your left," Sarah said.

I glanced over and saw Rebecca in the shadows. She pointed around the corner and then held up seven fingers. I nodded, and then she hurried off around the corner. *So, there's something we need to see, but does seven mean minutes? Or a group of people? Something else?* I wondered, glancing at Daniel.

Minutes? he mouthed.

I shrugged. If it was minutes, then we would have to figure out a way to leave our posts unnoticed. *We could just slowly back up, but there are probably too many cameras for that,* I thought, noting the security cameras as well as the many media cameras all around us. I was startled from my thoughts when the crowd burst into applause. The speaker was waving and slowly exiting the stage. I looked across and saw the other guards slowly following the speaker. *Ah, here's our chance.*

When we reached the shadows, Daniel and I hurried around the corner Rebecca had pointed at. The small hallway led back to a room behind the stage where three men sat at a table, their heads close together. *Could one of them be MAX?* I wondered, staying in the shadows. The noise from the crowd was still too loud to hear what these men were saying. Daniel took a picture with his watch and sent it to Sarah. "We may have found MAX," I muttered into my coms.

"Try to get me some good footage to send to Truth Squad," Sarah replied.

"Hey."

Daniel and I whirled around to face the commanding voice. A security officer stood behind us, his arms crossed and a scowl on his face. "Authorized personnel only."

"We have our badges," Daniel said, pulling it out of his shirt pocket.

The guard shook his head, snatching the badge from his hand. "Your uniforms do not authorize you to be in this area." He studied the badge, his scowl turning to concern. As he reached for the radio on his shoulder, it hit me. These badges weren't good enough to fool this guard, whoever he was.

I nodded at Daniel. We pushed past the guard, making a break for the crowd. The closest exit was behind the audience, and it was the fastest way to get lost from security. I could hear the guard calling for backup, but I didn't turn around to see if he was following. We had to get out, and fast.

I showed my badge to people as we ran through the crowd, most of the audience letting us through since we looked official. We made it out the back door and hurried to the nearest restrooms. We changed out of the guard uniforms and dumped them in the trash. I flushed my fake badge down the toilet, not wanting my picture to be left where someone could use facial recognition and discover my identity.

"You'd better get out of there," Sarah said. "There's a big group of guards looking for you."

"We're going," I replied as we ran out the bathroom door and toward the front exit. We found a space of fencing where no one was around and hopped the wall, then made our way back to the getaway car. As we drove off and my heartrate began to get back to normal, disappointment flooded me. *We could have been so close to discovering MAX. Instead, security now knows Daniel's identity.* I ran my fingers through my hair, frustrated. *And now my media internship is likely over, considering I totally ditched my post, so I don't have that source of info.* I sighed.

Daniel echoed my sigh. "That was a big fail."

"No kidding."

The next day, Daniel, Sarah, and I sat at the table eating breakfast in silence. We all felt it—miserable and stuck.

"I'm sorry, guys," Daniel said, shaking his head. "I shouldn't have handed my badge to that guard."

"That's not what made the mission fail, dude," I countered. "Honestly, if I had gone back to where the media crew had told me to wait, then I could've stayed undercover at the rally longer."

Sarah sighed. "You two can't change the past, and trying to figure out who messed us up isn't going to help us find MAX before it's too late. We need a new plan."

I nodded. "But where do we go from here?"

Daniel crossed his arms. "Well, I'm probably out of the picture now. They have my badge and can probably figure out my identity."

Sarah nodded. "So, Luke and I need to do undercover while you stay here as home base operator." Daniel nodded, and Sarah stared off into space for a second. "You know, what would really be helpful is a way to communicate with Rebecca safely. That would be the best, and fastest, way to gather the information we need."

"True, but how can we communicate without putting her or your brother at risk?" I asked. "If she gets found with an earpiece or any other listening device on her, she's probably dead meat." I jumped up and started pacing.

"Not necessarily," Sarah replied. "Rebecca has information MAX needs. Probably the codes Zaiden taught her. He can't get rid of her until he has the codes, and I'll bet she's doing whatever she can to stall giving him that info."

"We've got to work fast so that her stalling doesn't become her doom," I said. I stopped pacing and looked at my teammates. "I'm still not sure an earpiece or listening device is the way to go. So, what other options do we have?"

We finished breakfast in silence, everyone apparently not having any ideas. I stared out the window, watching a little family walk out the hotel to their car, followed by an elderly couple who were picked up by a taxi. The world outside seemed much too peaceful for the danger that lurked around the corner, a danger I wasn't even sure all the details of. Somehow that seemed more sinister than a mission I knew all the details of.

"You worrying over here, Luke?" Daniel asked, slapping my shoulder.

I looked back at the table, realizing Daniel and Sarah had cleared everything. "Yeah, sorry."

Sarah sat back down at the table. "'Be anxious for nothing, but in everything by prayer and supplication with thanksgiving let your requests be made known to God,'" she quoted.

"'And the peace of God,'" I smiled, continuing the verse, "'which surpasses all comprehension, will guard your hearts and your minds in Christ Jesus.' Philippians 4:6-7."

Daniel nodded. "I say we pray. We're stuck, but God isn't."

"And after we pray, I think we need to head to the store for more groceries," Sarah said.

I smiled at my friends, silently thanking God for them. "Sounds good to me."

Sarah and I decided to walk to the grocery store a little before lunch. Daniel would've gone with me, but Sarah was concerned that he needed to lay low for a while. Daniel also thought the walk would be good for both of us, since, according to him, we both would have "permanent worry lines from scrunching our eyebrows" if we didn't do something to loosen up. The fresh air did help. Something about cool autumn weather was energizing and put a smile on my face. I looked around at the shops as we walked. "Ooh, look—a doughnut shop!"

Sarah shook her head. "We're on a grocery run, not a doughnut run."

I shrugged. "Is there ever a time to skip doughnuts?"

"Before Truth Squad's annual physicals."

I rolled my eyes. "Way to be so practical, Sarah."

Sarah gasped.

"What—am I not supposed to call you practical?" I glanced at Sarah. Her eyes were wide with excitement.

"Look over there." She pointed across the street. "I think it's Rebecca!"

I looked where she was pointing. Rebecca was walking down the sidewalk on the opposite side of the road with a man about her height wearing a tan trench coat and fedora.

"Looks like they're headed for the sandwich shop," Sarah said as they walked inside.

"I'm suddenly feeling hungry for a turkey club," I said, nodding my head to the crosswalk.

We hurried down the street and crossed the road. Sarah called Daniel on her watch to let him know what was going on.

I opened the door to the shop. "Ladies first."

Sarah nodded as she stepped inside. "I do love a good sandwich."

The small shop was fairly crowded, probably the start of the lunch rush.

"Do you see them?" I asked.

Sarah shook her head and stepped in line. I looked at the round, bright yellow tables and the multi-colored plastic chairs around the room. There was no sign of Rebecca and her escort. I noticed a door leading to the connecting flower shop. "Let's check in there," I said, stepping out of line. Sarah followed me into the flower shop. It was smaller with less people crowded inside. The walls were lined with flower displays, and in the center of the room was a table full of small potted plants. Rebecca and the trench coat dude were standing in the corner with their backs to us, looking at the carnations.

"Sunflowers," I whispered, motioning toward the flower display next to the carnations. Sarah nodded and led the way. I stood next to the sunflowers with my back to Rebecca, trying to listen while Sarah examined the flowers.

"I found it," Rebecca said. I wanted to turn around and see what she found, but I retrained myself.

"Good," the man replied, his voice with a smooth British accent. "Read it."

I heard some paper crumple, then silence. *Come on, read it out loud,* I thought.

"Yes," was all Rebecca said.

"Ah, so he does want to meet. Very good." The man's British accent made me tense. So did a message about meeting with someone. I again felt the urge to jump in and tell Rebecca to stop moving closer to danger. I swallowed and prayed silently for strength.

"Did he give you a location?" the man asked.

"It does not concern you whether he did or not," Rebecca replied.

The man tapped his foot. "Don't play games with me."

"Read it for yourself."

The paper rumpled again, and after a second the man grunted. "It's some encrypted message, then. You wouldn't be so confident of this meeting otherwise. This message hardly makes sense."

"Would you leave a message in a public place without encrypting it, Mr. Roberts?" Rebecca asked.

I quickly typed the name into my watch and sent it to Daniel. Daniel replied quickly. "Need more than a last name."

Roberts cleared his throat. "Yes, well, we need to get going. Shall we purchase these?"

"Sure."

I waited for the two to walk past. "Let's go back to the sandwich shop and see if we can get a picture of Roberts as we walk past," I whispered.

Sarah nodded and led the way. As we walked past the checkout stand, she put her hand up to her hair and clicked a button on her watch, snapping a side profile picture of the agent.

Suddenly, Roberts turned around from the register, a bouquet of carnations in hand. "Now hold on there, miss," he said, a little too cheerfully. While his eyes were trained on Sarah, I quickly took another picture, this time capturing his whole face, and sent it to Daniel. "How strange—you look uncannily like my girl here." He motioned to Rebecca. I clenched my jaw, annoyed to hear another MAX agent refer to Rebecca as "my girl."

"Oh!" Sarah chuckled, then replied in a southern accent, "Why that's too funny! I've never met a doppelganger before!" She smiled brightly. "I love your accent. Where y'all from?"

Roberts frowned. "Well, I'm from the UK, but my associate is from the States."

"Oh, that's so cool! I've always wanted to visit England. All those castles are just so dreamy! Don't you think we should go sometime, honey?" Sarah said, looking at me.

I rolled my eyes and mimicked her accent. "Yeah, when money starts growing on trees."

She flung her hand out, bumping the bouquet of carnations. "He's way too practical—takes the fun out of everything."

I glanced at Rebecca. Her eyes darted toward the sandwich shop, and her face said to get going. "Honey, I think the line for the sandwiches is shorter now. Let's go eat." I nodded at Roberts. "Great to meet you. Enjoy your time in the great USA."

We got in line for sandwiches, and I looked back at the flower shop. Rebecca and the agent were gone. I sighed. "I hope we didn't blow it."

Sarah raised an eyebrow. "What do you mean?"

"Rebecca seemed rather nervous and was motioning for us to get going."

"Well, I think our conversation lasted just the right amount of time."

"What do you mean?" I asked.

Sarah tilted her chin up, a sneaky smile on her face. "While we were standing by the sunflowers and you were listening to the conversation, I removed the audio recording device and the location tracker from my watch. When I hit the bouquet, I dropped the devices in the flowers."

"So, the recording should be going straight to Daniel right now," I finished, grinning. "Great thinking!"

Sarah smiled. "Thanks!" She giggled. "I've always wanted to use a southern accent on a mission."

I expected to find Daniel listening to the audio Sarah dropped in the flower bouquet, but when we walked into our hotel, Daniel was standing in front of the TV, watching the news with his arms crossed and a scowl on his face.

"What's wrong?" Sarah asked, resting a hand on Daniel's elbow.

Daniel sighed and nodded at the TV. "That's what's wrong."

I glanced up. A picture of Daniel's face was on the news. "Dude! You're in the news!" I exclaimed, grinning at my friend. "That's cool!"

Daniel glared at me. "I'm not in it for anything good."

I looked back at the TV. The host was droning about who Daniel was—a private investigator from Oregon and part-time employee of Truth Squad. "Just before you got back, they had a phone interview with that guard we ran into," Daniel explained. "Lucky for us, there isn't any clear video to identify you. Everyone is trying to figure out what I was doing going undercover at the press conference. And now I'm in hot water."

"And so is Truth Squad," Sarah said. "This negative press isn't going to do us any favors."

"Well, this stinks," I said, running a hand through my hair. My mind raced. Daniel now couldn't show his face anywhere near our MAX investigations, and Sarah obviously looked way too much like Rebecca to keep walking around town without a disguise. The one good thing we had going for us was that Rebecca was staying put in D.C., making her easier to track. *What do we do next?*

CHAPTER 8

Matthew had a good scolding in store for us that evening. He critiqued us for not having better disguises and sticking with our original plan rather than going rogue. Mr. Truth encouraged us to lay low for a bit. He also told me to make sure I was thinking before acting, which stung. I'd heard that a few times in my Truth Squad career. And I was trying. But apparently not hard enough.

Sarah ended the video call with the president and vice president of Truth Squad and slammed the laptop shut. "Lay low? What—do they expect us to do nothing?"

Daniel shrugged. "Sounds like it."

"But we can't!" Sarah shook her head. "This is a time sensitive mission. The longer we delay, the more information MAX can get from Rebecca, and the closer we get to losing her, my brother, and failing the mission." Sarah stopped talking and looked away, blinking rapidly.

I sighed. "Sarah's right, Daniel. We can't do nothing."

Daniel threw his hands in the air. "And what exactly *can* we do? My face is now all over the news, and Sarah is Rebecca's identical twin."

"We work on using better disguises," I said. "You stay here to monitor what's going on, and Sarah and I can go undercover."

Daniel raised an eyebrow. "Go undercover? Where exactly do you plan to go undercover?"

I scratched the back of my neck, trying to think. "Well, I haven't gotten that far yet, but—"

"Exactly," Daniel interrupted, his face growing red. I'd never seen him this mad before. "This is exactly what Matthew and Mr. Truth said not to do. You're trying to jump into action without a plan."

"Boys!" Sarah stood up and planted her hands on her hips. Daniel and I shut our mouths. Sarah's tone meant business. "We cannot create any functional plan with the two of you arguing like this. Both of you need to go to bed, pray about it, and we'll make a plan in the morning. Got it?"

I strained to keep a straight face, surprised at Sarah's unusual commanding tone. "Yes, ma'am."

Daniel sat silently for a minute, rubbing his forehead. "I'm sorry. I shouldn't be taking this out on you, Luke. I just didn't expect to be the face of negative press for Truth Squad, you know?" He sighed. "You're right, Sarah. Let's start fresh with level heads in the morning."

Sarah walked around the table and gave Daniel a hug. "See you in the morning." She left.

Daniel nodded at me. "Really, dude, I am sorry. I was just as impulsive as you were, and I shouldn't have been so quick to blame you for everything that went wrong."

I clasped his shoulder. "I forgive you. And, honestly, Mr. Truth was right. I do need to work on thinking before acting."

Daniel went to bed, and I continued sitting at the table, staring out the window, not really thinking anything. After a while, I checked the location of the tracker Sarah had dropped in the bouquet. Not surprisingly, the location pinned to a dumpster a few blocks away from the flower shop. *Of course Rebecca would ditch the flowers,* I thought, slightly frustrated.

I went to bed, exhausted and needing answers. *Lord, give us wisdom and keep us safe—all of us.*

"I think I should go back to the JX headquarters."

I grinned as Daniel and Sarah's jaws dropped in unison. This definitely wasn't what they were expecting to hear from me first thing in the morning. Sarah put her coffee down on the table. "Really?"

"We couldn't get past the retinal scanner last time, remember?" Daniel said, shaking his head. "We couldn't learn anything important anywhere else."

"Maybe there's another way in besides the retinal scanner," I suggested, joining Daniel and Sarah at the table. "I think it's worth a shot."

"No offense, but this might be another acting without thinking plan of yours," Daniel replied.

I crossed my arms. "Well then, what ideas do you two have?" I smirked and waited as awkward silence filled the room. Sarah shrugged and Daniel refused to make eye contact. "I've been thinking about it all night, and I think if I have a good enough disguise, it won't hurt to go back and look for more clues."

"True," Sarah said slowly, squinting her blue eyes skeptically. "I'm just not sure how much more we'll learn from this."

I'm not really sure either, I thought, getting up and pouring myself a cup of coffee and adding a bunch of creamer. *But it's all I've got to work with so far, so it's better than nothing.* I also felt a peace about this idea, and I knew that God often provided peace when I needed direction in making decisions.

Daniel and Sarah pulled up the layout of the JX headquarters again and started looking for other entrances to the back half of the building. While they worked on that, I pulled out my suitcase and looked through the disguises I'd brought. I only brought one wig, a curly blond wig I hadn't worn since a high school play my freshman year. I tried it on and looked in the mirror. It wasn't as expensive as the wigs Rebecca used when she was a double agent, but it would do the trick. Since most of the employees I'd seen at the JX headquarters dressed up, I decided a button up shirt and dress pants were necessary to my disguise, as well as a little makeup to look older. I no longer wanted to look like a high-schooler—I needed to look mid-thirties.

After lunch, Daniel dropped me off behind the JX headquarters. "Remember our deal—if you don't find any helpful information today, we're coming up with a new plan," Daniel said as I jumped out of the car.

"Yup!" I saluted and marched toward the building. Daniel and Sarah had found a side supply entrance they thought I could get in through. I was wired with a listening device and camera, so if I found any clues, we would have them recorded. All I had to do was wait for a semitruck to arrive with a shipment and sneak in while it was being unloaded. Luckily, one was pulling in as I made my way to the entrance. I decided that the best course of action was to just casually walk in like I knew what I was doing. *Hopefully they won't question it and think I belong here,* I thought as I walked past the semitruck to the entrance.

I pulled on the handle to the door beside the truck. It was locked. I looked up at where the truck was backed up to the building. Somehow I'd have to get up there and get inside and still seem like I belonged there. *No sweat.*

Suddenly the door swung open. "Jack!"

I turned and found myself in a bro-hug with a complete stranger. "What's up?" I said, trying to hide my confusion.

"MAX said you wouldn't be here for another week," the guy said. He was dressed in sweats and his dark hair was a mess. He looked to be in his late twenties, and his hazel eyes glimmered as he winked. "I knew you would get it done faster than predicted, though."

I nodded. "Of course." *Who is this guy, and who am I supposed to be?*

"Come on in," the man waved me inside. I followed him in and waited for my eyes to adjust to the darkness. As I followed him down the hall, I sent a quick message to Daniel on my watch, "Find out who this guy is."

Daniel quickly replied, "Already on it."

"You're back just in time," the guy was saying. "MAX just called an impromptu meeting to give us a progress report. You can give your report now."

Oh, no. I don't even know who I am, let alone what job "Jack" was supposed to do, I thought. *How can I get out of this meeting?* Then it occurred to me—maybe I didn't want to get out of the meeting. *I might find out who MAX is.*

"What time is the meeting?" I asked.

"Well, we're technically already late," the guy said, shrugging as he looked over his shoulder at me. "But when are we not?"

Just then, Sarah piped up in my coms. "His name is Liam Hale. He has a degree in computer engineering, but that's all I've been able to find on him."

I texted back on my watch, "I need to know who I am supposed to be."

"Let's hurry. You know how much MAX detests being late," Liam said with a wink, pushing open a glass door to the outside. He took off in a fast walk.

"Uh, yeah," I replied, hurrying behind him. We were headed back in the same direction as before when Daniel, Sarah, and I couldn't get past the retinal scanner. *I may be fooling this Liam guy, but I can't fool a retina scanner.*

Daniel spoke into my coms. "Try to figure out what your last name is. 'Jack' isn't really searchable."

How do I do that without being awkward? I wondered. We were approaching a set of double-doors, and I could see through the glass a line of people, presumably waiting to get into the room after the retinal scanner. *I'm toast.*

"Let's take the shortcut," Liam said over his shoulder and started jogging.

I jogged after him, glancing around. *Where is this shortcut?* I noted security cameras at every door and window we passed. *So, Liam must do this often.*

Liam slowed down and headed toward a side door. A security guard stood just inside and pushed the door open. "Late again?" she said, rolling her eyes.

"Thanks, Amanda," Liam said as he rushed through. I nodded my thanks and followed him into a dark hallway.

Liam paused next to a metal door and took a few deep breaths. "Think he'll notice we came in this way?"

"Has he ever?" I asked with a smirk, hoping my confident reply was the right call.

Liam chuckled, relieving my tension. "Good point." He pushed the door open and stepped into a small closet with cleaning supplies. He put his ear up against the door on the opposite wall. "Sounds like people are still coming in. We're good." He opened the closet door and slid out.

I followed behind Liam. Looking around the room, no one seemed to notice that we'd entered through the closet door instead of the main door, which was right next to the closet. Obviously, Liam was often late enough that he'd figured out a secret passage into the conference room. *Rather ingenious.* I glanced at the conference table, unsure where to sit. I leaned against the wall, waiting for the table to fill so I would know where my place was.

"Jack!" A short, chubby man walked in the door and clapped my shoulder. "We didn't expect to see you back for another week." He guided me toward two empty chairs, so I sat beside the man, hoping that was Jack's usual spot.

Rebecca and Mr. Roberts, the British man we'd met at the flower shop, entered the room after that. They stood against the wall opposite me. Rebecca's eyes were scanning the room. She didn't seem to recognize me. *My disguise must be working, then.*

A hush fell over the group and Mr. Roberts stepped forward. "Ladies and gentlemen, I regret to inform you that MAX will be unable to meet us in person and therefore our meeting shall be conducted online." He pulled a remote from his pocket and clicked a button. The wooden panel on the wall lifted, revealing a large screen with a telephone symbol and the initials MAX below it. *Ah, man! I'm still not meeting MAX,* I thought, frustrated.

"Thank you all for meeting on short notice." MAX's deep voice boomed through the speakers. "Due to some unforeseen issues, I've called this meeting for a progress report. We'll start with Zack."

A man at the left end of the table opened a binder and started giving a financial report. The girl next to him gave a report on a construction project, but the details were given quickly and nothing she said gave away what this project was. As the reports moved around the table, I could tell there was some underlying plan all the details pointed to—finances, construction, media appearances, power grid tests, and so on. *It definitely relates to the whole power plant thing Zaiden had going,* I thought. *But what is the master plan?* I held my breath as the guy next to me gave a report on the function of the upgraded security. *What do I do? I don't know what Jack's job is—how do I give a report on it?* The man next to me closed his folder.

MAX cleared his throat. "Allen, what have your scouts learned about our opponent?"

I breathed a sigh of relief as the short, chubby man sat up straight and began his report. As I listened, I could tell that Allen's scouts were looking into the opposing candidate running for president. *Is MAX actually Jeorge Filips? Is he running for president? Or is he sponsoring him?* I wondered.

After the last report, MAX thanked everyone for the updates. "I must be off, but Roberts will fill you in on everything else you need to know."

"Wait—don't you want to hear Jack's report?" Liam spoke up.

"Jack?" MAX sounded surprised. "I was not informed that Jack had completed his assignment."

All eyes turned toward me. "It was, uh, unexpected, to say the least," I replied.

Rebecca, who had been staring at the floor with her arms crossed the entire time, darted her head up and looked at me, an eyebrow raised. I hoped her reaction was from recognizing my voice and not from sounding way off from Jack.

"I don't have time to hear it now, but I expect a full report by the end of the night," MAX said. "Goodbye." The call ended and the screen went dark. I breathed a sigh of relief. MAX hadn't noticed something off about "Jack." I wasn't sure how long I could keep up this charade if the meeting kept going.

Roberts walked to the front of the room and stood in front of the screen as the wood panels closed again. "Since MAX had to leave early, he asked me to fill you all in about some power failures and delays to the plan we've experienced." A few people started whispering, and Roberts snapped his fingers. Once the room quieted, he continued, "One delay is that we still have been unable to secure our location in Seattle."

Good, I thought, remembering back to when I worked undercover at the Patrick Brian Power Company. That was where I met Rebecca, who was also there undercover working for Zaiden. The small operation we'd planned to uncover fraud in the PBPC turned into a large-scale operation to take down Zaiden, a former assassin and partner with MAX. That operation led us to look into who MAX was and led me to be sitting in this conference room chair. Nothing would be more frustrating than to have our work in Seattle be undone now.

"Our plan to secure a location in Alaska has also been forfeited. We just don't have time to worry about that. We had an early power outage in the suburbs of Las Vegas, as well as in Harrisburg, Pennsylvania. We already have agents working to fix the bugs in Las Vegas, but MAX would like to send Liam, Sally, and Bob to Harrisburg to find out what went wrong and fix it immediately."

Liam groaned, but the other two agents nodded. "We'll get right on it," Sally said.

"You will need to get the bug fixed within the week, otherwise we will have to cut Harrisburg from the plan," Roberts said, his eyes narrowing. "And you know how much MAX hates cutting cities from the plan."

What plan? And why do they only have a week? When is "the plan" supposed to go down? I wondered.

"Are you sure we need to drop Anchorage?" Allen asked, adjusting his tie. "The more cities we drop, the less we'll be able to sway people."

Roberts shook his head. "We'd have to be ready within a month, and that is not enough time to hook up the power grid."

So, we have a month left. Not good. I glanced around the room, trying to fit the pieces together. *Power plants, major U.S. cities, a presidential election—what is MAX really up to?*

I glanced up at Rebecca. She was again staring at the floor, her eyebrows scrunched together and her fingers tapping against her leg. She was calculating something.

Chairs were starting to scrape, so I pushed mine back and stood up. *Maybe I can stop Rebecca on the way out the door—*

"Wait," Roberts said, and everyone halted. "Jack, since you're back early, would you give us your report?"

I froze. *I can't give a report—I don't even know who Jack is!* My mind raced as I tried to think up an excuse. "Uh, well..." I coughed. Suddenly, my phone rang. *Thank You, Lord!* "I'm sorry, I've got to take this." Everyone nodded at me knowingly, and I quickly stepped out the door.

I pulled my phone from my pocket and answered Daniel's call while hurrying down the hall. "Perfect timing."

"We've still got no leads on who Jack is, so I knew I had to get you out of there."

"Everyone seems to have great respect for whoever Jack is, and it seems like he's not around often. I'm wondering if he's a higher-up with MAX," I said quietly.

"The other thing I was wondering was if Jack does something similar to Braxton and Ethan," Daniel replied.

"A hitman?"

"Yeah. It would explain him being gone for unknown amounts of time."

"True. I'll see if I can catch Rebecca alone and find out more info on who I'm supposed to be. It's hard to act a part when you have no clue who you are."

"Jack!" The security guard next to the retinal scanner waved as I walked through the door. I nodded and waved back. *Man, everyone knows this Jack guy.*

"I'll hang up. You try to get information from Rebecca and keep me posted," Daniel said, and hung up.

I found a corner at the end of the hall to stand in where I wouldn't be too conspicuous and kept my phone in my hand to look busy while keeping an eye out for Rebecca. Finally, I heard a British accent headed down the hall.

"I want you to stay here until I get back. No funny business."

"I haven't caused any trouble the entire time I've been here. Why would you expect me to do anything now?" I could almost hear Rebecca rolling her eyes.

Roberts huffed. "I know MAX has put a lot of faith in you, but I know better than to trust the likes of you."

"You know exactly why I'm cooperating with MAX," Rebecca replied, almost growling at the man. "I will not jeopardize the life of my brother through funny business." She paused. "Unlike you."

I glanced up. The two were standing directly in front of me. Roberts hands were in tight fists and his face was red. Rebecca kept staring Roberts in the eye, a scowl on her face. Finally, Roberts huffed and marched off. "Ten minutes," he called over his shoulder.

Once he was out of sight, Rebecca relaxed. I cleared my throat and she turned to face me. "Luke?" she whispered.

I nodded. After a couple agents walked past, she came and leaned against the wall next to me. "What in the world are you doing?" she whispered.

"Thought I'd drop in for a visit," I replied, grinning.

Rebecca didn't look pleased. "Do you know how dangerous it is for you to be here, and to pretend to be Jack of all people?"

"Do you know how dangerous it is for you to be here?" I retorted, trying to hold back my frustration.

"MAX can't kill me without the information I have, and I won't let him have it until he proves my brother is safe. So, we're at a stalemate."

"Rebecca, MAX has way more leverage than you if he's holding your brother hostage." I paused while a security guard passed, then whispered, "Do you know where your brother is? Maybe we can break him and you out."

Rebecca shook her head. "That's part of the problem."

"And you're sure MAX has your brother?" I asked.

She nodded. "I've been on several conference calls with MAX, and my brother has been with him."

"Is your brother working for MAX?" I asked skeptically. From the little I knew of Isaac, it didn't seem unlikely for him to be involved in this type of scheme.

"I did wonder about that," Rebecca replied, looking less confident. "But he's done some signaling during our conference calls. From what I've gathered, he started working for MAX, but when he realized MAX's full plans, he was going to quit working for him. That's when MAX kidnapped him."

"Did MAX know you were related when he hired Isaac?"

"I think so."

"So, the entire time Isaac was working for MAX, it was really just a matter of time before MAX would use him for leverage to get you out here anyways." I shook my head and took a deep breath, trying to control my anger.

Rebecca sighed. "As much as I hate to admit it, I think it's a good idea for you to keep up this Jack charade. It might help us find Isaac sooner."

I smiled. "Perfect. Then I can keep an eye on you, too, since you keep losing every tracker we give you."

Rebecca rolled her eyes. "Kinda have to. They're all paranoid here that I have some way I'm getting information back to Truth Squad. So, I've got no phone and have to get rid of any trackers I find." She smiled. "That's why the flowers went in the garbage." Rebecca checked her watch. "Roberts is going to be back in two minutes."

"Okay, so fill me in on Jack. I have no clue who this guy is. I dressed up like this to sneak in with the delivery guys, and Liam decided I was Jack," I explained.

Rebecca looked surprised. "Well, you need to have Sarah do your makeup exactly the same every day, then, because you look almost perfect."

"How'd you know Sarah did my disguise?" I asked, trying to look offended.

"Wild guess," Rebecca replied with a wink. "The agent you're portraying is Jack Pierre. He's a hitman, and he actually works pretty closely with MAX."

"Daniel guessed that one right."

Rebecca looked nervous. "From what I've heard, Jack never communicates with MAX when he's on a mission. He'll just disappear for a while and show back up when the job is over. That's why he's kind of a legend around here—he's the best guy MAX has."

"No wonder everyone's treating me like a cool dude," I said, impressed by how much power this one guy held.

"Luke, don't you get it?" Rebecca asked. She was visibly worried, which made me worry since she normally hid her concern. "Luke, if Jack comes back, you're dead."

I took a deep breath, the gravity of her statement hitting me like a semitruck. "Okay. I understand."

Rebecca sighed. "I see Roberts coming. You'd better go." She grabbed my hand and squeezed it.

I nodded and hurried down the hall and out a side door. "Daniel," I spoke into my coms, "find whatever you can on Jack Pierre."

The next day I was back at the JX headquarters, again disguised as Jack. The night before, Sarah and Daniel looked into Jack Pierre. There wasn't too much they could learn other than the high-school and college he graduated from. He had a business degree, and that was as much as we could learn about the guy. We weren't surprised, though, considering his occupation as a hitman.

When I walked up to the side entrance, a security guard immediately opened the door. "Good morning, Mr. Pierre," he said.

I nodded and hurried inside. *Good thing he didn't ask for a badge or ID,* I thought, looking around. I wasn't sure what Jack did when he wasn't on a mission, and I needed to figure that out quickly. I also needed to figure out a report to get to MAX, a report on a mission I knew nothing about. *Even if I knew what Jack's mission was, I have no clue how to reach MAX,* I thought.

Mr. Roberts made his way over to me, Rebecca following close behind. "Good morning, Jack. I trust you've rested well from your last assignment."

I nodded. "I have."

He stepped closer and lowered his voice. "I've heard from MAX, and he's slightly put out that you haven't sent him your report yet. I know it's hard to recover from the extreme time zone changes, but I would recommend you get on it."

"My apologies. I was rather exhausted," I replied.

Mr. Roberts cleared his throat. "Well, I must be off to take care of some business. Since MAX hasn't reassigned you yet, I could use your assistance."

"Of course." I took a deep breath, wondering what this assistance might be.

"I need you to keep an eye on Miss Sanders," Roberts continued. I suppressed a smile as Rebecca rolled her eyes. "She has valuable information MAX needs, and we cannot lose her." He glared at Rebecca.

"Understood."

"I should be back by noon, and then I could use your assistance in another matter at that point." Roberts spun on his heel and hurried away.

Once Roberts was out of sight, Rebecca relaxed her stance and grinned. "How perfect. You have to be my chaperone till noon."

I grinned back. "Could not have worked out better, praise God."

"We need to start with getting your report to MAX," Rebecca said, heading down a hall to the right. "There's a small conference room this way that should be empty."

"Do you know what Jack's mission was?" I asked.

"Not really. I overheard MAX tell Roberts something about going overseas and making a stop in Hawaii before heading back here. But, of course, they haven't heard any updates from Jack this whole time." She pulled open a door and peeked inside. The lights were off. and no one was around. "This will work." She flipped on the light, and I followed her inside.

I noticed a security camera in the top corner of the room and turned on a disabling unit I carried on my belt. It would cause static on any listening devices and make the camera blink off so long as it was more than four feet from me, that way my coms would still function properly. It was an invention Matthew and I had worked on for several years growing up, and now it paid off as Truth Squad agents.

"Daniel," I spoke into my coms, "see if you can find any news stories from Hawaii that might help us."

"On it," he replied.

Rebecca tapped on a black doughnut shaped computer in the middle of the table, and the screen activated, a glowing hologram screen directed by hand signals. A password box popped up. "I'll work on the password while Daniel looks up news stories," she said and began her hacking work. I watched quietly as Rebecca worked, feeling relieved to be able to work with her again.

"I'm not finding any out of the ordinary news stories," Daniel said.

I tapped my chin, thinking. "Well, if the real Jack is still off on his mission, then he probably hasn't completed it yet."

"Or he keeps these things really well hidden, even from the public."

"True."

"What's Daniel found?" Rebecca asked, looking up from the computer.

That's right, she doesn't have coms, I remembered. "He hasn't found anything so far."

She thought for a minute. "Well, if Jack hasn't completed the mission yet, that could be good for you because you'll have more time to work undercover."

"Yeah, but what do we do when he gets back?" I asked.

"We intercept him," Daniel replied.

"How are you intercepting this guy? If he's such a legend, how would we find him?" I asked.

"I can call up Matthew and get some more Truth Squad agents out here. We show them what your disguise looks like, and they can keep an eye out for a match."

"Sounds risky."

Rebecca giggled. "Luke, when have you ever cared about being risky?"

I grinned. "Good point, but D.C. is large enough that it would be really challenging to find a guy who looks like my disguise without actually having his picture for facial recognition or something."

"I'm in," Rebecca said, the hologram screen on the table expanding. She pulled up a generic email and typed up a short message to MAX about the mission being completed smoothly with no tracks. "Sound good?"

I proofread the email and nodded. "It's rather vague, but I think it's our only option."

We sent the email and then she deleted the evidence of us using the computer before shutting it down.

"Well, that's one problem solved. On to the next one," I said, sitting down at the table.

Rebecca sat down beside me and checked her watch. "We've got two hours."

"So, you give us whatever information you can as fast as you can, and then we work on locating Isaac. Sound good?" I asked.

"Wait a minute, I don't think looking for Isaac is going to help with shutting down MAX, will it?" Daniel asked, but I ignored him.

Rebecca nodded. "What do you need to know?"

"Well, the most pressing question is—who is MAX?"

"Well, unsurprisingly he has several identities. But he is most well known as the millionaire J. Xavier, but he's also known as Jeorge Filips," Rebecca explained.

"Wait—MAX is running for president?" Daniel asked.

I relayed the question to Rebecca, and she nodded. "Yes, but that's also an alias. I still haven't learned what his real name is. Everyone here calls him MAX."

"Hmm. If we ran facial recognition on some of his presidential speeches or something, would we find his true identity?" I asked.

"I'm on it," Daniel said.

Rebecca shrugged. "I doubt it will work, but it's worth a shot."

I leaned back in my chair and stretched. "Okay, so what have you learned about this plan MAX has?"

Rebecca sighed. "From what I've gathered, the plan is to cause a mass power outage across the U.S. MAX has been getting his men into as many major city power plants as he can so that when the power shuts off—"

"He has the control needed to make everything right, which means everyone will want him to become president," I finished, my eyes widening. Rebecca nodded. "Wow. That's insane. But why not run for president the normal way? Why go to all these years of trouble securing power plants and stuff?"

"Continued control," Rebecca said with a shrug. "If people try to plan an uprising against him, he has the power to stop them because too much of our American way of living requires power."

I rubbed my forehead, trying to wrap my brain around what MAX was up to. "How much of the U.S. will go dark if he succeeds?"

"I'm not sure. He wanted to make the entire thing go dark, but since we destroyed Zaiden's EMP and stopped a lot of the powerplant takeovers, he isn't going to be able to do it the way they had originally planned. He's been unable to secure another EMP since then."

"Wait a second," I said, my jaw dropping. "Are you saying that four years ago when we stopped Zaiden's operation, they were planning this U.S. takeover thing for that presidential cycle?"

Rebecca nodded and crossed her arms. "We had no clue what we were getting into."

I sat in shock for a couple seconds, my mind racing through all the wild things we'd been through the past four years because of this MAX operation. I shook my head and got back to the next pressing question. "Why does MAX need you?"

"You remember all those codes Ethan was trying to learn from me?" she asked. I nodded. "Well, apparently, Zaiden didn't fully trust MAX with the entire plan, so some of the plan for orchestrating this power outage is only possible through the codes he taught me, and the codes have to be in the proper order to work. If MAX has the code, then he can make the power go out over all of the U.S. simultaneously, otherwise he has to manually shut the power down in every city. Zaiden also had it worked out with these codes so that it would be nearly impossible to restore power to each city if MAX uses this switch off code without using the same code to switch them all on again, but I'm not sure how that works." She sighed. "But if he can figure out the codes, then he would have even more power because he could do the whole power outage thing whenever he wanted to with Zaiden's code, and no one would be able to stop him."

"So, MAX can carry out his power-outage-takeover plan without the codes, but he doesn't want to." *Rebecca is so sure that MAX needs her, but he doesn't really. He just prefers this plan,* I thought, a sinking feeling in my stomach. *She has even less leverage than I thought. This is not good.*

Daniel cleared his throat. "Rebecca's right, the facial recognition just brought up Jeorge Filips."

A wild idea popped into my head. "Rebecca, what if we sneak you out of here while Roberts is gone?"

Rebecca lowered her eyebrows. "No. My brother dies if we do that."

"Okay, so we have a little less than two hours to find Isaac and sneak both of you out. You have enough information from being here to turn MAX and this whole operation in to the FBI."

Rebecca pushed her chair back and stood up, crossing her arms. "It's unlikely that we'll find Isaac that quickly. I've got no clues as to where he is. He might not even be here. He could be at any of the locations MAX has."

I stood up and grinned, hoping to ease the tension. "It's worth a shot. Let's get going." I opened the door to the conference room and peeked out. No one was nearby. I took a step out into the hall, but Rebecca pulled me back into the conference room. "Where is the most likely spot for someone to be held captive?" I asked, trying not to be frustrated with her.

"I told you—I have no leads." Rebecca looked very frustrated.

I turned to look her square on. "Rebecca, we've got to do something. This is seriously dangerous for you to be here, and the longer you're here the more dangerous it becomes. The closer MAX gets to needing to manually switch off the power, the closer you get to being dead."

She glared at me. "The longer you stay here pretending to be Jack, the closer you get to being dead, and your death would be a lot sooner than mine."

"Why don't you sneak out and get all your info to Truth Squad and the FBI? If we work fast enough, we can rescue Isaac and—"

"It's not that simple!" Rebecca interrupted. She pulled up the sleeve on her black shirt, revealing four stitches down her forearm. "I've got a tracker in my arm. If I leave this building without Roberts or MAX or someone that MAX has authorized, my brother dies." Her eyes began to water, and she quickly looked away. "It's also a shock device, so I probably would die, too. I thought I had the upper hand, that if I played my cards right, did all the manipulation things I've been trained to do—" She choked up and shook her head, whispering, "I put far too much confidence in my training, and it's backfired."

I pulled Rebecca into a hug, that way she couldn't see the anger and worry on my face. *Another layer of difficulty.* My mind raced through the options—remove the tracker, which would risk injuring Rebecca's arm, or find some way to block the signal; but, without the right equipment, I wouldn't be able to do that. *God, give me strength and wisdom.*

Rebecca pulled back from my hug and wiped a stray tear from her face. "I suppose we can do some looking around and try to find clues before Roberts gets back."

"That's the spirit," I replied with a smile. I glanced down the hall, making sure the coast was still clear. "But let's pray first."

CHAPTER 9

Rebecca gave me a tour of the building before Roberts got back. I had only been down the hall on the left off the courtyard, which I learned was the only way to the conference room I had been in the day before, aside from Liam's false closet that I filled Rebecca in on. Down the right hallway were several smaller conference rooms and offices. There was also an elevator at the end of the hall. There were two basements and then twelve floors above us. The basements and the top four floors all required special passcodes to enter.

"Have you tried decoding any of the passcodes?" I asked as we took the elevator up to the eighth floor.

"No, I've always had a guard following me around."

"Yeah, we can never be too careful with the likes of you," I teased. The elevator door opened, and we stepped out into a dimly lit hall. "I take it people aren't up here much."

She shook her head. "Floors seven and eight are where they keep clothing items for the storefront. The rest of the floors below are all used for MAX's operation. It's a very odd layout."

I poked my head inside some of the unlocked doors. Sure enough, clothing racks with suits and tuxedos filled the rooms, and the shelving units were stuffed with shoe boxes and ties. "Have you looked for stair access to the top four floors?"

Rebecca nodded. "No luck. If there is stair access, then it's behind a locked door."

I grinned and pulled a small plastic box from my pocket. "Good news—I never leave home without a lock pick set."

"Only because I told you not to after that one mission." She winked.

"Why focus on those minor details?" I said, returning the wink. I handed her one of my lock picks. "You take the left doors. I'll work on the right."

The first door I unlocked opened to a room of tuxedos, and based on the locks on the hangers, I figured these were very expensive. I moved on to another door and found a computer room. I stepped inside and the lights switched on. *Motion-sensor lights. This is definitely the security room,* I thought, noticing the hundreds of screens displaying the different rooms in the building. An alarm sounded and a red light started flashing from the ceiling. *And I've tripped something.*

I relocked the door and pulled it shut. "We'd better go," I whispered to Rebecca.

She closed the door she'd just opened. "What'd you do?"

"Found the security room."

"We can't take the elevator. That's where the guards will come from. We've got to find the stairs," Rebecca said.

We continued trying doors. Each room I looked inside was full of boxes. "We'll just have to hide," I said, opening the last door on my side of the hall.

"Wait a minute," Rebecca said. "I think I found it."

I followed her into the last room on her side of the hall, glancing at the elevator lights. The doors were getting ready to open. I quickly closed and locked the door behind us. I turned around and saw another room full of boxes. "I thought you said you found the stairs," I whispered.

"I did." Rebecca pointed across the room. As my eyes adjusted to the darkness, I saw what she was pointing at—a door in the far corner. "Let's go."

We tiptoed through the room to the door. I ran my hand along the edge of the door, feeling for any sort of alarm that would go off if we left through the staircase. Sure enough, at the top of the door I felt a magnetic plate. "Do you think there's anything magnetic around here?" I asked.

"I'll look." Rebecca started tiptoeing around the room. I studied the plate. It was screwed into the door, and there was zero gap between the plate and the sensor on the doorframe. *So, I could unscrew the plate and keep it up against the sensor while Rebecca slips out the door, but then how do I get out without setting off the sensor?* I looked closer at the sensor. It was built into the doorframe, so there was no chance of removing it without removing the entire frame. *Someone really doesn't want people going upstairs.*

"Someone's coming. Get down!" Rebecca hissed.

I hit the ground as the door swung open and light poured in. I held my breath, waiting for footsteps. *Rebecca's on the other side of the room. If they come in, she's toast,* I thought, panicking.

"Nothing here," a woman said. "I think our security malfunctioned again."

"Well, I'll check the video one more time to be sure," another guard replied. The voices faded as the door swung shut.

I breathed a silent prayer of thanks that the guard didn't enter the room, and that my camera disabling tool was working properly. I stood up slowly. "Rebecca, you good?"

"Yup."

I jumped at the voice by my side. "Don't scare me like that."

"Sorry. I just thought it would be better cover back here than near the door," she replied. "I couldn't find anything magnetic."

"Well, I can unscrew the panel and we can get out, but we probably can't close the door without it falling and going off."

"Roberts will be back any minute. Let's just wait for the security guards to leave and then take the elevator."

I raised an eyebrow. "Shouldn't someone always be in the security room? Why was it empty, and won't they stay in their posts now?"

Rebecca shrugged. "Maybe this is a secondary security room. Anyways, we risk that, or we risk the alarm going off on the stairs."

I thought for a minute. "Well, since I'm the legendary Jack, I'm guessing the better bet is being seen by the guards. I can talk my way out of trouble better in that scenario." *I hope.*

We waited a minute by the door, and then I slowly pushed it open. The hallway was empty. Since none of the doors had windows, I knew that we could get back to the elevator no problem. *But if a guard comes out of the security room, there will be a lot of confusion,* I thought, knowing my camera blocker would keep us invisible.

We hurried down the hall and Rebecca pushed the down arrow. Time crawled as we waited for the elevator to reach the eighth floor. I kept my eye on the security room. Just as the elevator dinged to signal its arrival, the handle turned on the security room door. "Hurry, someone's coming." I pushed Rebecca inside and spammed the close door button. A guard stepped out of the security room just as the doors were closing, and I couldn't tell if she saw us or not.

Rebecca breathed a sigh of relief. "That was way too close."

"But we found the stairs," I replied. "Maybe we're a step closer to finding your brother."

The rest of the day passed uneventfully. Roberts seemed to relish dominating "Jack's" attention and gave me another tour of the building, and this time I kept my camera blocking device off. Roberts spent most of his time complaining about little details to the building that needed improvement. I took note of the boldness with which he critiqued MAX. That, along with leading the meeting the day before, made me think he was one of MAX's top guys. *Having an in with this guy could be useful,* I thought, trying to think of the positives rather than be annoyed listening to Roberts complain all afternoon.

I left that evening slightly frustrated by Roberts, but hopeful. If he trusted me to keep an eye on Rebecca once, hopefully he would do it again and we could get some real work done.

I picked up hamburgers on my way back to base. I swung the hotel room door open and grinned, holding up the takeout bag. "I'm starving! You two ready to eat?"

"Sure." Daniel's reply was unenthusiastic.

I glanced between him and Sarah, my smile fading. Both looked rather stressed. "What's up?"

Sarah shook her head. "More news coverage on Truth Squad, and it's not good coverage. Daniel's face is everywhere."

I nodded, unsure whether my friends needed a listening ear or distraction from the bad news.

Before I could make up my mind what to say, Sarah patted Daniel's shoulder. "There's not really anything we can do about this right now, so why don't we eat?" She smiled at me. "You and Rebecca did great work today. If you can keep investigating like you did today, we'll finally get some real leads."

While we ate, I filled Daniel and Sarah in on the details of my day, telling them about the layout of the building, giving a few names I'd heard for them to research, and explaining our theory on where to look for Isaac.

I finished my briefing, and Daniel cleared his throat. "Luke, Sarah, this might be hard to hear, but I think looking for Isaac should be the least of our concerns right now."

"But if we find Isaac, we can get Rebecca out of danger," I replied, crossing my arms.

Daniel straightened his shoulders. "Getting Rebecca out of danger is important, but stopping MAX is more important to the millions of Americans being threatened with a tyrannical government."

"But if we get Rebecca out of there," Sarah quietly replied, "we can keep MAX from having the codes he needs."

"You heard Rebecca—he doesn't need the codes; it just helps him have more power."

"But it will buy us time. If he's that power-hungry, he will wait until the last minute to try and get those codes."

"But when is the last minute?" Daniel shook his head. "We can't waste time."

"It's not wasting time," I argued, an unexpected growl in my voice. I jumped up from the table and began pacing, my arms crossed and my jaw tense. I took a deep breath, praying for anger management before responding. "Daniel, in looking for Isaac, we may be able to find MAX. He is the leverage MAX is holding over Rebecca. MAX is probably staying close to Isaac, keeping him under heavy guard so there's no way Rebecca could rescue him on her own."

Sarah nodded, keeping her eyes trained on the floor. "We may have more leads looking for Isaac than waiting around for MAX to show up," she whispered.

Daniel sighed and ran a hand through his disheveled hair. After a long silence, he nodded. "I just think we all need to be careful. We have invested interest in this mission. I mean, Sarah is Rebecca's twin; Luke, you're dating Rebecca, and I'm dating Sarah. We're all closely connected to this mission, and, I hate to say it, but that might be part of our weakness."

I glared at Daniel, wanting to come back with a clever retort. I couldn't. His words hit deep. *Lord, I know he's right, but I don't... I can't not care. This mission, we've been trying to solve it for four years, and... it's Rebecca...* My prayer trailed off as I stared out the window, mindlessly counting the cars in the parking lot.

"Maybe we should talk to Mr. Truth," Sarah said quietly. I glanced over to see her quickly wipe a tear from her face. "If he thinks we're too invested, he can send reinforcements... or replacements if it has to be."

"We can't get a replacement for Luke—he's our look-alike." Daniel rested his chin in his hands.

"I don't want a replacement," I said firmly, sitting back down at the table. "But Sarah's right. We should discuss how things are going with Mr. Truth. When are we supposed to give the next update, anyways?"

"In two days," Sarah replied. "Until then, let's keep doing what we're doing. Let's pray for wisdom and clarity, and let's get some sleep so we're ready for tomorrow."

"Hey, Jack!" Liam called across the parking lot when I arrived the next day.

I waved. "What's up?"

Liam jogged to meet me on my way in. "Man, Roberts hardly let me get a word in with you yesterday. He's so controlling, am I right?" He rolled his eyes.

"Classic Roberts." I copied Liam's eyeroll, hoping my response was in character for Liam's good friend.

"I'm surprised you're still here," Liam said, pushing open the door. "Normally MAX has you in and out quickly."

I nodded. "Roberts will keep me busy till then."

Right on cue, Roberts walked over to us. "Jack, good morning. If you could come with me, please."

I gave a nod to Liam and followed Roberts to a conference room. My heart pounded. *Did he find out I'm not Jack? Or learn about Rebecca and I sneaking around?*

"Have a seat," Roberts said, and I did. "I contacted MAX last night." He paused, and I braced myself for bad news. "He doesn't have an assignment for you yet, so I got permission to have your help in a couple things I'm working on here."

My shoulders relaxed and I slowly nodded, trying to play it cool. *What would an important dude like Jack say?* "I heard as much from MAX."

A glint of jealousy flashed in Roberts eyes, and I knew I'd said the right thing. "Yes, well," he coughed. "My tasks are time-sensitive, so we need to get started right away. I have a meeting in ten minutes I'd like for you to attend. It will fill you in on our work. I'll fill you in on what you and I will be doing after the meeting."

I nodded and leaned back in my chair, raising an eyebrow. "I notice your charge is not with you today."

Roberts huffed. "No, I can't afford to babysit today. But don't you worry—everything is secure. She won't be getting away."

I kept my eyebrow raised but didn't say anything. Roberts squirmed, then mumbled about checking on things and left the room.

"Well done," Daniel spoke into my coms. "I think you're getting the hang of this."

"Try to get as much info as you can from this meeting," Sarah said, and I could hear keys clicking in the background.

Roberts came back into the room, his arms crossed and eyes narrowed. I tapped my fingers on the table. A couple of awkward minutes passed, then the door opened, and three guys walked in.

The four men discussed power plants around the country, pulling up a holographic map that showed in green the plants under their control and in red the plants they still needed access to. I smiled with satisfaction, noticing the old power plant Rebecca worked at was still in red.

"I don't think we can secure all of these before the deadline," an older man with a gruff voice said, shaking his head. "I think we need to pick the priority locations and let the rest go."

"That is not an option," Roberts almost yelled. "MAX intends to have all of these in his possession for the full effect of his plan. So, do whatever you must do to make sure that we have them secured—get more men to join you, take more drastic measures, whatever!"

The men divided up the different power plants between them. The older man still looked doubtful, but kept his mouth shut until Roberts dismissed them.

"Don't come back until your task is complete!" Roberts said as the men left.

The older man rolled his eyes and mumbled, "Then don't expect me back."

Roberts huffed as the door slammed shut. "I despise having to work with him."

"He's probably right," I said, nonchalantly checking the time on my watch. Roberts looked ready to protest, so I changed the subject. "Now, I notice you did not choose any power plants to secure. What is our assignment?"

"Good observation." Roberts sat down at the table and tilted his chin up condescendingly. My face twitched as I held back a laugh; this guy really did not like Jack. "We have a more important matter to attend to here in D.C. You know—"

The door swung open, and a lady poked her head in the door. "Roberts, Pierre, I hate to interrupt your meeting, but it's urgent."

Roberts sighed impatiently. "What is it, Emily?"

Emily stepped inside and swung the door closed. She was dressed professionally in a suit dress and held a clipboard. "I have a report from Derickson that a malfunction occurred with switch number forty-nine this morning at six-thirty." She handed the clipboard to Roberts. "The malfunction has been resolved, but both Chesapeake and Norfolk, Virginia lost power for over an hour."

Roberts glanced at the clipboard. "Just tell me the bad news."

"Reported suspicion of malicious intent has already begun circulating, and police detectives are on the case to find the culprit. If you'll look at page three," Emily gestured to the clipboard, "you'll see that there is evidence leading them to D.C. MAX requests you send agents out immediately to intercept the detectives. I have a press-release to write for MAX to leverage the situation."

Roberts waved his hand at her. "Of course, I'll get the agents sent. And get an alternate story to Austin right away."

"Yes, sir." Emily turned and walked out the door.

I closed my eyes for a second to control the excitement trying to break out in my eyes. *I hope Daniel and Sarah heard all that.*

Roberts cleared his throat. "Well, Jack, it seems my original plan will have to wait. I need you on the trail of the detectives."

My heart skipped a beat. *Oh, no.* "Okay, I can do that." *How will I do this?*

Roberts slid the clipboard to me. "Read through that and pick your man—or several, whatever you think you can get done by tomorrow afternoon."

"Tomorrow afternoon?" I asked, my mind zooming through everything I knew about Jack. "Sorry, but no. I work at my own pace."

"Not this time. You must—"

"I will return when the job is done," I said, standing and walking to the door.

"Wait, you can't take the whole packet. There are five detectives—you can't go after all of them."

I stopped with my hand on the doorknob. *Do I say I can? Or is that way overkill? Normally it would be. But if I don't go after them, then someone else will, and these detectives might be killed. God, what do I do?*

Roberts pulled at the clipboard from under my arm. "I can get Liam on a couple guys—"

I straightened. "No, I prefer to work alone." With that, I pulled the door open and walked out of the building.

CHAPTER 10

"What are you thinking?" Daniel asked into my coms.

I opened my car door and slid behind the wheel. "I'm thinking I'll stop for coffee and a doughnut on my way back. Want anything?"

"Are you out of your mind? You just agreed to take out five police detectives! And now you have to finish that mission before you can get back in undercover."

Sarah cleared her throat. "You probably shouldn't stop for coffee when you have that clipboard in your car."

I laughed. "I wasn't going to stop—I'm going to a drive thru." I started the car and pulled out of the parking lot.

Daniel sighed. "Luke, you may have just jeopardized our one way of solving everything."

"You don't know that," I shot back, anger creeping into my voice. I took a deep breath, not wanting to argue with my friends. "I should be back in thirty minutes."

I took out my earpiece and put it in my pocket. *God, I seem to have found myself in another predicament. But I don't know what else to have done. What if letting someone else track down a detective resulted in that detective's death? But Daniel is right—if things go wrong, what if I jeopardized our mission? God, I need Your help.*

I found a coffee and doughnut shop on my way home and got everyone's usual orders. I almost ordered a fourth Mexican mocha for Rebecca out of habit. I felt a pang in my heart, remembering once again that Rebecca was in danger, and I was not there to protect her. *Lord, keep Rebecca safe.*

Sarah greeted me with a half-smile when I entered with the coffee and doughnuts. Daniel's arms were crossed, and his face was even crosser.

"I got you both the usual orders," I said, setting the coffee tray and doughnut box on the table.

Daniel ignored the food and glared at me. "You need to think before you act."

"I did think. That's why I took the whole clipboard. These guys might've been killed if I didn't take the whole clipboard."

"And a lot more people will be in danger if we fail at this mission!" Daniel exclaimed, stepping in front of me. "Take it seriously, dude. This is about so much more than five detectives."

The anger I was holding back behind my smile burst out. "What—do you think I'm not taking it seriously? My girlfriend's life is on the line, here. Our entire country has it coming for them if we don't succeed. Take it seriously—I am! Dude, just because I care about the individual lives of these detectives doesn't mean I'm not taking it seriously."

"Hey!" Sarah's yell caught me off guard. Sarah didn't yell often. Daniel and I spun to face her. She swallowed and her eyes glistened as though she were holding back tears. "I know this is a high-stress situation for all of us. But we can't do anything if we're fighting in our own ranks. We need to work in unity. Both of you take your snack and... and... I don't know, go to opposite rooms or something. I have a call with Mr. Truth in five minutes to give him an update, and I don't need to talk over you two arguing." The corners of her mouth drooped, and a tear slid from her eye. She dashed into her room and softly closed the door behind her.

I grabbed my coffee and doughnut and left the hotel room. Sarah was right—we needed to be unified, but I needed to calm down so I could think straight again.

After a quick run on the treadmill in the workout room, I went to the lobby to eat my snack. I found Daniel already in the lobby, staring out the front sliding door with a half-eaten doughnut in hand. I thought about turning around and going back to the workout room, but seeing the droop in Daniel's shoulders changed my mind. I walked up and sat in the green chair beside him.

"Sorry for exploding back there." I ran a hand through my hair, blinking back the unexpected tears in my eyes.

Daniel shook his head. "I shouldn't have said you weren't taking things seriously. I'm sorry too."

"Why are you in the lobby? Aren't you supposed to be laying low?"

Daniel shrugged. "It isn't too busy right now, so I figured I was okay." I raised an eyebrow. "I know, I shouldn't be out here. But I get tired of feeling helpless." He stood. "Want to take the stairs?"

Back at our room, Sarah waved us over to join her call with Mr. Truth. Daniel and I sat down at the table, and I filled Mr. Truth in on the current situation with the detectives.

"Well, that was probably a risky move," Mr. Truth said, rubbing his hand along the back of his neck. "But I think you did the right thing. Sarah sent us the files, so we can get in touch with those detectives and start working together on this case. You were right to not agree to the time frame Roberts gave. That should buy us some time to figure out some way to coordinate with these detectives so that they stay safe, and you can get back to work undercover."

I nodded. "What should we do while we wait, then?"

"We'll need you to meet with these detectives once we locate them, so stay alert for that. And, Daniel, make sure you keep staying low. Truth Squad has been getting negative press, and we've even had a few protests outside our campus." Mr. Truth sighed. "I want to tell you to stay safe, but the stakes are higher on this mission than on any other mission we've done. We need to stay alert."

"Yes, sir," Daniel said, nodding gravely.

"Also, since we're coming down to the wire, I think it's time we send in some backup. Matthew and I will be joining you as soon as we're able." Mr. Truth glanced at his watch. "I need to get going. I'll contact you as soon as we get in touch with the detectives. Before I go, let's pray." Mr. Truth bowed his head, and we all followed suit. "Lord, we pray for peace, protection, and wisdom over this mission. We pray for truth and righteousness to prevail and for evil to be thwarted. In Jesus' name, Amen."

The next day crawled by like a caterpillar taking a snack break every three steps. We didn't have anything to do since we were waiting on word from Mr. Truth. Daniel looked up some of the news articles circulating about Truth Squad. The story of Daniel's appearance at the rally had grown elaborately, and many articles claimed that Truth Squad was an agency secretly forcing conversions to Christianity, which was obviously not true if anyone had taken the time to research Truth Squad's mission statement. Sarah ended up asking us to stop reading the negative press because we were getting too worked up over it. So, we sat around the table and waited for word from Mr. Truth, Sarah reading a book, Daniel staring grimly out the window, and me tinkering with a broken wrist-computer, trying hard and failing to not think about Rebecca and being undercover to help her.

Finally, after what felt like forever, a message alert dinged from the laptop. Sarah set her book down and read the message. "Good news—four of the five detectives have been contacted, but they haven't been able to get ahold of the fifth detective, Eaton. It seems that he is going old school, not using any electronic or radio devices, so he's been hard to track. He's been seen around this area in the last twenty-four hours, and Mr. Truth wants us to locate him."

"Let's do it!" I exclaimed, jumping up from my seat. *Finally, something to do!* I grabbed the files on the detectives and found Griffin Eaton. He was fifty-six years old, five foot nine, and missing a hand from a farming accident as a young man. The picture showed a man with silver hair and a beard and bright green eyes.

"Where was he seen?" Daniel asked, looking over Sarah's shoulder.

"A traffic camera got a picture of him in his car when he ran a red light on Shady Grove Road, near the university." Sarah turned the laptop so we could see the picture of the car and license plate. The car was a forest-green mustang, and the license plate read 92A83Z.

"Looks like he ran the light at 1:32pm," Daniel said. "We can use the traffic cams to find out where he went after that."

About fifteen minutes later, Daniel located the last traffic cam that spotted Detective Eaton. A couple blocks from the JX headquarters, he turned down a side street out of view from the cameras and never exited onto another road.

I raised my eyebrows and nodded in approval. "This guy is good. He's almost made it to HQ."

"Let's have you two head out to where he was last seen, find the detective, fill him in on our work, and then you'll be ready to go undercover tomorrow," Daniel said.

"I think this is a mission for Jack Pierre," I said, jumping up and running to my room to get my disguise.

"Not really," Sarah replied.

I put on my curly wig and came back to the group. "Well, Jack did agree to take out five detectives."

Sarah shrugged and Daniel rolled his eyes. "Whatever. If you feel like dressing up, then do your thing," he said. "Now get going."

We drove to the street the mustang turned onto and parked along the side of the street. Red brick apartment buildings lined both sides of the street. I hopped out of the car and looked around. Several vehicles were parked along the street, but no green mustang.

I joined Sarah on the sidewalk. "I guess we should locate the mustang first."

Sarah nodded, and I led the way down the street. The road came to a dead end, but we found tire tracks going farther on.

"Do you think he hid his car back in those trees?" Sarah asked.

I shrugged. "Possibly. It won't hurt to look." We followed the tracks into the grove of bright orange and yellow trees. If we weren't on a mission, I would've loved to stare at the bright colors and enjoy the carpet of fire-like leaves on the ground, but I forced myself to focus on the tire tracks we were following. A ways back into the forest we found the green mustang, surrounded by trees and sprinkled with leaves. No one was around. We peered through the car windows, and we saw a sleeping bag in the back seat as well as a bag of food.

"Looks like he's planning to camp out here," Sarah remarked. "If he's coming back here, maybe we should just wait here for him."

The sound of crunching leaves filled the air. "Maybe we won't have to wait long," I whispered, darting behind the trunk of a tree. Sarah found another hiding spot and we waited, listening. I listened to the sound of the leaves crunching. There wasn't a distinct, two-step pattern. *Either this is an animal, or there are two people headed our way.*

"Hey, you brought the mustang!"

My eyes widened. The excited voice sounded familiar. I glanced around the tree for a second to see two men by the mustang—the detective, and Liam Hale. *Why is he here? And why is he with the detective?*

"My ride of choice," the detective replied, his voice deep and with a southern accent.

I messaged Sarah on my watch. "Stay low. Liam is with the detective." Sarah nodded in reply.

"So, whatchu got for me?" Detective Eaton asked with an I'm-getting-comfortable sigh.

"Not much," Liam replied. "MAX still isn't back, Jack was sent out on another mission, and Roberts has been quite nervous ever since Jack showed up."

Is Liam an undercover cop? I wondered as Liam gave the detective a brief run-through on the cover-up Roberts did for the malfunction in Virginia.

"Well, well, well, ol' Jack still intimidates him?" Eaton said with a chuckle. "Maybe that will give us an advantage."

"How so?"

"If Roberts still feels like he's competing with Jack, he'll get sloppy. Of course, Jack has never cared for Roberts and won't get sloppy on his account."

"I still think you should reconsider Jack."

"Why?"

"He only works for MAX for the money, but the moment MAX slips up, you know Jack will be out," Liam explained. "And I think he's starting to get fed up with MAX, too."

My watch vibrated. I looked down and read Sarah's message. "Maybe these guys could help us."

"If Jack is loyal for the money, we won't be able to persuade him to be loyal to us. We don't have the resources he has," Eaton said.

"But if he thinks this is a sinking ship, he would jump with us," Liam argued.

So, it's not in Jack's character to team up with these guys because he's basically a bounty hunter. But that means I still have to get rid of the detective somehow. I peeked out from behind the tree at the two men. *We've only got one option.* I sent Sarah a reply: "We need to kidnap Eaton."

My watch buzzed. "What's the plan?"

"You go back to the car and wait for the mustang to drive by, then follow us back to the hotel. I'll make sure Eaton drives us there."

"Okay."

I waited for Sarah to start making her way back to the car, listening as Liam and the detective continued discussing what was going on with MAX's operations. It was obvious these two were being cautious; they could sense the nearness of MAX's plans coming together, but they kept saying they didn't want to act too soon.

I glanced out from my hiding spot to see where the two men stood. Liam sat on the hood of the car and the detective leaned against the driver's side door opposite my hiding spot. With his back to me, I knew I wouldn't be spotted by Eaton, but Liam's perch on the hood facing the detective meant I would need to be careful to avoid his peripheral vision.

Slowly, I crept from my hiding spot toward the car, staying low. There wasn't a whole lot to keep me hidden between my tree and the car, and I cringed with each step as the dry, fall leaves crackled beneath my feet. A slight breeze picked up, ruffling the leaves in the treetops and helping my slow steps to blend in.

"Well, how long will you be here investigating?" Liam asked.

Eaton grunted. "As long as I need to until we can clear our names and get this wrapped up."

Liam yawned. "Well, I guess I should head out. Are you camping here for the night again?"

"Nah, someone around here was complaining about a homeless man camping in these woods, so I figured I should find another spot. I'll let you know where I set up."

I crept up to the mustang and slowly grabbed the handle to the passenger side door, staying low and praying Liam would stay focused on his conversation. Slowly, I pulled the handle, waiting for the door to release. It didn't. *It's locked. Rats.*

Liam hopped down from the hood of the car. "Well, then, take care. I'll see you when I'm able."

Leaves crunched as the two men walked away. I stayed crouched by the back tire, waiting for Eaton to come back and unlock his car.

After millions of seconds passed by, I heard the crunch of steps headed back my direction. I grabbed the door handle again. The steps neared, and I held my breath, waiting. Finally, the lock clicked inside the door. I quietly pulled the handle and opened the door just enough to wiggle into the back seat, pulling the door closed as quietly as possible. I slid onto the floor of the vehicle and waited, my heart pounding, praying that Eaton hadn't seen or heard me climb into the back seat.

The driver door opened, and Eaton slid inside with a sigh. I could hear the rhythmic bubble sound of texting. After a minute, the whir of a seatbelt followed by a click reached my ears. The car roared to life and Eaton took off. I sent Sarah a message: "Heading out."

Eaton came to a stop and turned up the country music playing on the radio. Slowly, I sat up and slid into the seat behind Eaton. He took a right from his stop at the stop sign, headed in the opposite direction of our hotel.

"Wrong turn," I said, trying to keep my voice low and menacing.

Eaton gasped and swerved, then glanced over his shoulder. "Jack?" His eyes were wide. He looked petrified.

I held back the smile trying to burst out over Eaton's facial expressions and repeated myself. "Wrong turn."

"Why are you here?" Eaton's voice shook behind an angry façade.

"You know exactly why I'm here, so either turn around or risk the consequences."

"Fine." Eaton whipped the car into a U-turn and headed back the way he'd come.

"Good. I'll let you know when you need to turn." I was rather enjoying this intense character.

After we passed back by the neighborhood we'd left, Sarah pulled out behind us. After making several turns and checking the rearview mirror each turn, Eaton started fidgeting. "We're being tailed."

"I know."

"Don't you think we should lose them?"

"No."

Eaton raised an eyebrow. "So, you have an accomplice?"

"For today." I hoped my nonchalant answer was good enough. Jack was a mysterious character, but one thing that everyone knew was that Jack worked alone.

"Where are we going?" Eaton asked.

"Turning right at the next intersection."

"That's not what I meant."

I grinned. "But that's all you need to know for now." I returned to my straight face. "If I were you, I would avoid asking too many questions and just drive."

Eaton closed his lips firmly and made the right turn. For the rest of the ride to the hotel, he never said a word.

Once we reached the hotel, I told Eaton where to park and launched into my instructions. "Now, do exactly as I say. You will follow me into the hotel, and we will take the elevator to the third floor and walk down the hallway to room 326. You will walk with me and carry on a friendly conversation the entire way. My accomplice will be following behind and if you do not follow my directions to the letter, you can expect my accomplice to make short work of you. Understood?"

A smug look came across Eaton's face. "Ah, the accomplice keeps you from having blood on your hands."

"Understand?" I repeated, raising an eyebrow. Eaton sobered and nodded. "Then exit the car." I pushed my door open and waited for Eaton to do the same before stepping out.

We walked together through the front doors of the building, and I jumped into the first small talk I could think of. "So, what's your favorite doughnut flavor?"

Eaton's shocked look quickly vanished as the doors opened again behind us. He quickly punched the up arrow for the elevator. "Uh, maple bars."

"Classic choice," I replied, following him into the elevator. Eaton moved to turn around, but I quickly whispered in his ear, "Stay facing the wall until I say otherwise." Eaton nodded. I turned to look at Sarah and nodded for her to push the third-floor button.

We were silent for the ride to the third floor, once the doors opened and Sarah had stepped out, I said, "Exit the elevator and head to your left."

Eaton did as he was told, continuing the conversation about doughnut flavors as we walked. Once we reached room 326, Daniel swung the door open and ushered us inside.

Eaton's jaw dropped as he stared at Daniel. "Wait a minute—I've seen you on the news! You're that Truth Squad guy."

"Take a seat," Daniel said, motioning to the dining table chairs. "This explanation will take a while."

"Jack, why are you working with these people?" Eaton asked, sitting down as directed.

"Daniel, make sure we don't need to worry about any listening or recording devices, and make sure the detective is unarmed," I said, ignoring Eaton.

Once we had Eaton's gun and all his electronics, Sarah took her post by the door, and Daniel and I sat down to explain things. "Well, let's get the most awkward part out of the way," I began. "I'm not Jack."

"Nuh-uh." Eaton crossed his arms. "You're not fooling me."

"Really, I'm not. My name is Luke Mason, and I'm working undercover for Truth Squad."

"You mean, Jack has been a fake name all this time?"

"No, I mean I was mistaken for Jack, and that got me into MAX's headquarters."

Eaton was thoroughly confused now. "So, you've caught the real Jack?"

I shook my head and pulled my wig off. "Nope. It was a misunderstanding that has been quite helpful, actually."

"Here's the deal," Daniel said, "we're working to take down MAX's operation, and we are getting very close to doing so. Part of that has been Luke working under cover as Jack. MAX assigned Jack to take out five detectives who were getting on his trail, and we've been able to work with the other four to let them in on the situation and get them to safety. That is what we are now doing with you."

"However," I jumped in, "I do know that your name is connected with MAX, and when his ship sinks, you will go down with him." Eaton squirmed but didn't say anything. "So, if you help us with any information you know, we might be able to help plead for a lighter sentencing for you when everything's all said and done."

Eaton glanced between the two of us and sighed. "I knew this would catch up to me eventually. But if this is the way it has to be, I'll take it." He looked me in the eye and shook his head. "But I'll warn you, kid, once the real Jack gets back... you're dead meat."

Eaton agreed to giving us all the information he knew in exchange for a shorter sentence. He used to work for MAX, doing cover-ups for him whenever law enforcement got onto his trail. However, six months ago he didn't do a good job with his cover and was kicked out. Liam was also fed up with MAX because no matter how good his work, he could never get higher in the ranks. Recently, they decided to get revenge. Liam was leaking MAX's plans to Eaton, and once they had enough evidence to get an investigation started on MAX's company, Liam would quit and erase the two's information from MAX's computer systems. It really did seem like a good plan, except for the fact that they were nowhere near ready for an investigation to start. And time was running short.

Throughout Eaton's confession, he continued to remind me that I was dead meat once Jack returned, and I had no clue what I'd gotten myself into. "Even MAX is afraid of Jack. If he wasn't, he wouldn't pay him so much money," Eaton said. "No one wants to be on his bad side, and you're already a mile past that."

We turned Eaton over to the proper authorities and sent all the info he'd given us to Mr. Truth. At that point it was ten o'clock, so we headed to bed.

My mind raced as I lay under the covers, staring at the sprinkler on the hotel ceiling. I wasn't surprised that Eaton said I was dead meat, but I still felt the weight of it pressing me deeper into the bed. The possibility of going rogue and rescuing Rebecca and forgetting about the rest of the mission floated through my head, but I quickly batted it away. I knew we would be on the run from MAX forever if I did that, and this mission was too important to jeopardize. *But Rebecca's important, too,* my mind screamed. I sighed and prayed, *Lord, help me to stay focused and alert, and keep Rebecca safe. I know You can do that much better than I can.*

The next morning, I was again disguised as Jack and back at the JX headquarters. Even though I arrived at eight, everyone was bustling around as though they'd been there for hours. I spotted Emily who had given us the report about the detectives and walked over to her, keeping a confident stride.

"Emily, I need a conference with Roberts. Where is he?" I asked.

She looked up from her clipboard. "Good morning, Jack. Roberts is currently in a meeting with MAX."

"Well, then could you give him the message that his assignment is completed."

Emily nodded. "Right away." She hurried off down the right hallway.

I leaned against the wall and looked around for a few minutes, watching people go here and there, some carrying clipboards, others carrying boxes, others dressed to the nines and walking like they had somewhere important to be. Rebecca was nowhere to be seen, but that didn't surprise me. I assumed she was with Roberts. Remembering he was with MAX, I quickly prayed again for her protection.

Maybe I could look around for Isaac while I wait on what to do next, I thought, glancing around. *No one will question what I'm up to since they're all afraid of me.*

I walked over to the elevator and pressed the up arrow. My plan was to go back to the eighth floor and find a way to get up the staircase. The elevator dinged and the doors slid open. I stepped inside and pressed the button for the eighth floor.

"Jack!"

I glanced out the door and saw Liam waving at me. I held the door open and waited for him to join me.

"MAX is calling a meeting with us," Liam said breathlessly, stepping inside. He hit the basement 2A button.

Is this for real—am I meeting with MAX face-to-face? I wondered, taking a deep breath to control my excitement. *Interesting that we're meeting with him on the lowest floor.* The elevator descended quickly, and the doors slid open, revealing a dimly lit metal hallway with a guard posted by each of the four doors leading to the double-doors at the end of the hall.

Liam jogged to the end of the hall, and I followed close behind. He flashed his badge, and the guard swung the door open, not bothering to ask me for my badge. *That's a relief,* I thought as I followed Liam inside.

Inside the large room was a massive amount of high-tech equipment. I forced myself to act nonchalant and not stare at the hologram computer on the far wall, just calling my name to geek-out.

Liam turned to face a large wooden desk on the left side of the room. I stood beside Liam and again fought to contain my expression. The desk was ornate and looked super expensive with its gold-embellished carvings of eagles, hawks, and other birds of prey. I forced myself to look up from the desk to the man sitting behind it. The presidential candidate Jeorge Filips and millionaire J. Xavier, in the flesh. Even with a three-piece suit, I could tell he was buff, with dark hair and eyes and a perfectly trim mustache. On the front of his desk sat a gold and ivory name plate. Morton Andrew Xavier. *MAX.*

"I have a mission for you two."

CHAPTER 11

"I need the two of you to plant this chip," MAX held up a small black square pinched between his thumb and forefinger, "in the electrical box of the capitol building."

I raised an eyebrow. *Infiltrating the government?*

"Now, Jack, I know this isn't what you normally do, but I need you on this one. This is a very sensitive operation, and you're the best man for the job." MAX leaned forward on his desk. "Trust me, it will be worth your efforts."

I nodded but kept a skeptical expression on my face. "Where is the electrical box?"

"What is the chip for?" Liam asked.

"This one is to gain control of the electricity in the capitol—"

"There's more than one?" I interrupted.

"Yes," MAX said, glaring at me, his eyebrows raised. *Hmm, maybe interrupting is out of Jack's character.* MAX pulled another black chip, with three gold stripes across the back, from the desk drawer in front of him. "This one will be put in the computer monitor of the Senate majority leader. This gives us access to not only his computer but every monitor in the House and Senate galleries. And, before you ask," MAX continued, holding up a hand, "these chips have been tested, and we know they won't be detected by anti-malware devices or online security searches."

"What's our deadline?" Liam asked, crossing his arms.

"Two days." MAX turned to me. "I need you back for another mission by then, so two days is all we can afford." He opened the folder in front of him and slid the two chips into a gray fabric bag stapled inside the folder. Closing the folder, MAX stood and pushed the folder across his desk. "I trust I will hear a positive report from the two of you in two days."

I nodded, picking up the folder. "Yes, sir."

As Liam and I exited the basement, Daniel spoke up in my coms. "Let us know as much info as possible. We'll need to foil this operation somehow."

"But that will ruin Luke's undercover work," Sarah argued.

The two went back and forth, but I ignored their arguing. They were both right—we couldn't let MAX have this access to the government; it was one step closer to his takeover. But failing would easily jeopardize my ability to work undercover, the only leverage we had.

We took the elevator back upstairs and found an empty conference room to go over our file. Liam plopped down in a chair and yawned. "What's in the packet?"

I sat down in a more dignified manner and looked through the file. "We've got two maps, one of the area surrounding the capitol, and the other of the capitol itself." I slid the maps over to Liam. "Here's the instructions MAX just went over." I flipped through a few pages that explained how to insert the chips and instructions on storing the chips in the provided bag since it would keep the chips from being detected while going through security. It also explained that the chip had to be inserted in the senate majority leader's computer only, because, based on the information MAX uncovered, it was the most likely monitor to gain access to everything else. "Looks like a fairly simple job, so long as we don't get caught."

Liam nodded. "The hardest part—especially at the capitol. There's a lot of security. I mean, visitors aren't even allowed in the House and Senate galleries, and neither of these maps tell us where the electrical box is. How will we locate that without suspicion?"

"We have two days. We have time to do our research." *And time to figure out how to make this plan fail while still maintaining my cover.*

"Ah, the lovely capitol." My eyes swept across the concrete walkway up the grand stairs and white pillars to the white dome and the bronze Statue of Freedom. The stars and stripes waving in the breeze seemed small on the front of such a grand building. I felt like I should pause to salute or something, but a quick glance at Liam reminded me of my mission. Plant some chips, but also get caught.

We'd spent the afternoon before planning. None of our research helped us locate the electrical panel, so we decided the first plan of action would be to locate that panel. Once that chip was taken care of, we would sneak into the House gallery and plant the second chip, then leave as quickly as possible. I had planned to go back to the hotel and debrief with Daniel and Sarah after making our plan, but Liam had suggested we drive to the capitol at night when there would be less traffic, stay in our car, and get an early start at the capitol so that we would have extra time to find the electrical panel. I wasn't sure what the real Jack would do, but I didn't want to draw any suspicions, so I agreed to his plan.

For the past twenty-four hours, I had not been able to directly communicate with Daniel and Sarah. I occasionally heard updates from them, but I couldn't reply. I didn't know what their plan was, but I hoped it would keep MAX from his goal and still keep me undercover.

"Where do you think we should start our search for the electrical panel?" Liam asked, leading the way toward the building.

"The panel will probably be somewhere inconspicuous," I replied. "Somewhere that doesn't interrupt the façade of the building, and somewhere people won't easily get to."

"So, it's most likely going to be inside."

I nodded. "Let's play it safe, though. You look around inside, and I'll check the perimeter of the building. We'll be more efficient that way."

Liam stopped walking and turned to face me. "If we're going to be efficient, why don't you take care of one chip, and I take care of the other?"

That would be an easy way for him to get caught and blow the mission, I thought. I paused to see if Daniel or Sarah would make any comments, but my coms were silent. "But finding the electrical panel is going to take longer than planting the chip in the Senate gallery. And once that's done, we'll need to get out of here. The security around there will probably be much greater than at the electrical panel."

Liam shrugged. "I think we should do it."

I rolled my eyes. "Fine." I slipped the chip for the Senate out of my sports jacket inside pocket and handed it to Liam.

Liam's eyes widened with a hint of nervousness. "Wait, you're not doing this chip?"

"Nope." I started walking toward the building again. "Get in and out as fast as you can. We have our coms—let me know when the mission is complete."

"But... don't you think you should, you know, do this one? I mean—"

"You wanted to split up." I whirled around to face Liam, keeping my voice stern. "We're splitting up. Now get on it."

I continued my march toward the capitol. My coms were completely silent, both from Liam and Daniel and Sarah, the entire walk up to the grand staircase. Instead of going up, I made my way around the edge of the building. I kept my eyes trained on the clean, white surface before me, watching for any change in surfaces to hint at the existence of an electrical panel.

Liam's voice buzzed in my ear. "I'm inside."

"Good," I replied.

I continued walking the perimeter of the building. The longer I walked, the more confident I felt that the electrical panel wasn't on the outside of the building. It was probably also somewhere secure, away from visitors. *But where?* I made it to the back side of the building, the sprawling green lawn and bright orange trees popping against the white building. I darted behind trees and passed both sets of stairs, not finding any sign of an electrical panel. *I wonder where the backup generators are kept. And why wouldn't MAX have us do something about that, too?* Thinking about MAX brought my mind back to Rebecca. Somehow I needed to make it back to MAX with a good alibi for why this mission failed. *Lord, give us wisdom.*

Back at the front of the building, I decided to head to the visitor center. It was in the basement, and a basement seemed a likely candidate for electrical panels. I walked back across the concrete walkways, past the glass floors looking into the visitor center, and down the stairs and turned to walk through the cased opening into the visitor center. I made my way through security, then headed to the stairs leading down to Emancipation Hall. As I started down the staircase, I looked up and noticed the tunnel leading to the Library of Congress. *That seems like a good spot.* I hurried back up the stairs and through the tunnel doors. The tunnel certainly wasn't the cool, underground feeling I hoped for; instead, I walked down a white-walled hallway with two rows of canned lighting and linoleum flooring, walking through several doorways as I followed the signs pointing to the Library of Congress.

"We have a plan," Daniel's voice buzzed in my ear.

I couldn't reply without Liam also hearing, so I held back the "finally" that tried to escape my lips.

"Keep going down the tunnel until you round the corner, and stop at the third picture frame on the wall. Wait there until Agent Holton stops and says '17:17.' He'll have a green ballcap on. Slip him the chip and then you have fifteen minutes to get out of the capitol."

I picked up my pace and rounded the corner past the gold lettering and arrow pointing me to the Library of Congress. I stopped and looked down the hall. Picture frames lined both sides, going every other one in a zig-zag pattern. *Does three mean three picture frames on the right side, or three going back and forth from right to left?* I decided to go simple and just count three on the right, stopping by a collage of pictures and quotes.

I leaned against the wall and looked around. A young family followed by an old veteran walked past. It wasn't too busy in this tunnel. *I wonder how far underground this tunnel is. Or how long it took to dig this thing. I mean, there's multiple tunnels, so—*

"Seventeen-seventeen."

I pulled my thoughts together and glanced at the man next to me who'd said the passcode. He wore a lime green ballcap, jeans, and a t-shirt, but I noticed he had an earpiece. I slipped my hand into my jacket pocket and grabbed the bag. I passed the chip to Agent Holton, and he slid it into his back pocket. With a nod, he made his way down the tunnel to the library of congress.

I turned and headed back to the visitor center. "The chip is planted," I said into my coms, knowing both Liam and Daniel could hear me. "Meet me at the car when you're done."

"Okay," Liam replied, a hint of surprise in his voice. "I'll be there soon."

I hurried outside and made my way toward the parking garage at Union Station, resisting the urge to turn around and stare at the capitol and take it in.

As I stepped onto First Street, an alarm sounded in my coms. "We've got trouble," Liam said.

"What's happening?"

"There's an alarm on this computer, but the chip is in place." Just then, a bunch of muffled yelling came through the coms. I glanced at my watch. I had five more minutes to get out of the area. I started on a jog down the street.

I pulled out my earpiece connecting me with Liam and threw it in a trashcan as I passed by. Once I got to the parking garage, I ran to the stairwell and hurried up two flights. I pushed the door open and stepped into the dimly lit third level.

"Get on the ground, this is the FBI!"

My heart dropped. Suddenly, I was surrounded by FBI agents. *How did they know I was here?* I dropped to the ground and waited quietly as I was handcuffed.

"What is happening? This wasn't part of the plan," Sarah said anxiously.

"I'm contacting Mr. Truth right now," Daniel said. "There must be some mistake."

A memory flashed in my mind of Daniel, Matthew, and I talking after our undercover mission in Colorado. "Or a mole," I muttered, hoping Daniel heard. *Daniel was right; MAX must have agents in the FBI.*

I found myself in an interrogation room, handcuffed to a table and staring at a two-way mirror. My coms were confiscated, along with all the gadgets I had on me. Somehow my wig was still on me, which confused me since the FBI knew I was working undercover. It had been three hours since my arrest, and not much had happened. An hour ago, an FBI agent came into the interrogation room, but I quickly asked for a lawyer before she could say anything. That at least bought me a little time, since I now could not be interrogated without my lawyer. I prayed Mr. Truth was getting through to the FBI. *But if they know I'm undercover and that word gets to MAX's mole, then I can't keep being Jack. I'll be toast.* I sighed, tapping the metal table to the tune of Old MacDonald. *I need to get out of here and back to my role as Jack,* I thought, frustrated. *The longer I sit here, the more danger Rebecca could be in. Lord, please intervene.*

The interrogation door creaked open, and an officer escorted a man in a gray suit and black tie. A tall, big man with brown hair. He gave me a crooked smile. "Mr. Pierre," he said, extending his beefy hand.

I grinned at my friend. *Matthew.* "Good to see you."

Matthew nodded as the officer released my handcuffs from the table. I was escorted to another interrogation room, this time without a two-way mirror. I was again handcuffed to a metal table and Matthew sat opposite of me. *You'd think I was super dangerous the way this guard is acting,* I thought. The guard kept a close eye on me and seemed tense, like he expected me to be up to something. *Then again, they do think I'm Jack Pierre.*

Matthew kept his eyes trained on the officer until he left. "Okay, let's get down to business," he said, pushing a button on his watch. "Alright, cameras are disabled." He pulled out a metal pin from his coat sleeve and quickly picked the lock on my handcuffs.

"Finally!" I shook my wrists out and jumped up. "Do you know how uncomfortable it is to be handcuffed for three hours?"

"I don't." Matthew shrugged. "But we need a plan to get out of here. Mr. Truth is working with Agent Brandon to get everything sorted out, but you don't have enough time to wait for things to settle down. Plus, the mole in the FBI could be alerting MAX to your undercover role, and we need to stop that if possible."

"So, we have to figure out who the mole is before I can go back undercover?" I asked.

Matthew nodded. "Mr. Truth also learned that the computer chip that was confiscated when Liam was apprehended has gone missing. My guess is the mole has it and is either returning it to MAX or completing Liam's mission."

"Either way, we can't let that happen." I glanced around the cinderblock room. "What's the plan? I mean, how am I getting out of here in the first place, and how do we find a mole in such a large organization?"

"Well, the plan for getting you out is simple." Matthew pulled off his suitcoat and dropped it on the table. Matthew unzipped a hidden inner pocket on the back of the coat and pulled out a full FBI uniform. "You change into this, and your outfit and wig will go back in the pocket. When the coast is clear, we'll walk out of here and wait for a commotion when they realize you're gone. That commotion should buy us time to find the chip, and hopefully our mole."

A minute later I had transformed from Jack into an FBI agent. Matthew pulled an infrared detector, a five-inch black cylinder with a sensor on one end and computer screen on the other, from his belt and held the sensor to the door. Gray waves slid across the screen as the sensor scanned for body heat through the door. After thirty seconds, the screen flashed green.

"Coast is clear," Matthew whispered, turning the door handle.

I followed Matthew into the hall. We didn't have to worry about being seen by the cameras since Matthew had his camera disabler turned on.

"We need to check the security footage to see when the chip went missing," I said as we hurried away from the interrogation rooms.

"Exactly what I was thinking." Matthew stopped his speed walking and stepped up against the wall as several agents walked past. "I'll message Mr. Truth for a layout of the building." He typed up a message on his watch, then continued his march down the hall.

I followed behind stiffly, every muscle in me ready for a commotion that was bound to happen once someone discovered Jack was gone. A minute later, Matthew got the layout of the building from Mr. Truth and located the security monitoring room. We took a left turn down another hallway and took the stairs up to the second floor. As we entered the second floor, an alarm sounded. Matthew and I made eye-contact and nodded in unison. It was time to get moving.

We hurried to the end of the hall, swimming upstream from all the agents rushing for the stairs. The hallway turned left at the end, and the next door was the security room.

Matthew peeked inside the open door. "There are two agents inside."

"I'll go in. You stay out here." Without waiting for a response, I squared my shoulders and marched into the room. I had an idea.

The nearest FBI agent, a middle-aged man with a diet coke in hand, looked up at me over his glasses from his chair. "Did you hear about the assassin disappearing?" he asked, his voice deep and scratchy.

"I did," I replied, walking up to a free monitor. The monitor was already running, rotating screens between different security cameras. "I'm looking through recent footage to find where that lawyer went."

The man grunted and took a sip of his coke. "It figures someone who would be so elusive for so many years would have a so-called lawyer ready to help him escape."

"No kidding."

I started looking through earlier video footage, backing up three hours to when Liam and I first arrived. I knew the computer chips had been put in an evidence room; I'd seen a lady with gloves examining the chips when we were brought inside. Once I figured out which camera focused on the evidence room, I watched the footage on triple-speed to discover when the chip was taken. I skipped through forty minutes of the lady examining the chips and everything that was confiscated from Liam and me. For twenty more minutes, the room was empty. Then, the door opened and in walked a man with a green ballcap. *Agent Holton? No way.* He walked around the table, picked up a couple gadgets, and then swiped his hand across the table like he was brushing off crumbs. With that, he left the room, one of the two computer chips now gone. *No wonder MAX has pulled out just in time for every Truth Squad operation we've done. Agent Holton works next to Agent Brandon; he always knows what we're up to.* I took a deep breath to hold back my excitement. I switched cameras to follow Agent Holton's trail from the evidence room. I skipped through an hour of Agent Holton talking with other agents, and then followed his progress around the building through the third hour. At the time the alarm sounded, he made his way out of the building to the parking lot. I checked the parking lot cameras for his vehicle. He got into an open top black Jeep with the license plate AA12B7. After repeating the number to myself several times, I switched the monitor back to current video footage.

"Did you find anything?" the middle-aged agent asked.

I shrugged. "Yup." I didn't wait to come up with a story and hurried out the door.

Matthew looked up from his crossed arms, perched against the wall next to the door. "Got it?"

I nodded. "To the parking lot."

Matthew led the way back to the staircase. "So, who is it?"

"Agent Holton."

Matthew stopped and whirled to face me, his eyes blazing. "Seriously?"

I nodded. "He swiped the card, and when the alarm went off, he took off in a black Jeep."

Matthew shook his head and continued down the stairs. "Brandon's not going to believe it. Holton has been working with him for a while now."

We hurried outside and Matthew pointed out his ride, a deep blue pickup truck.

"We need to track down a black Jeep with the license plate AA12B7," I said, hopping into the passenger seat.

Matthew took off his watch and handed it to me. "Contact Sarah."

I nodded and sent her a quick message. "I sure hope we can get my gadgets back from the FBI. They took some good tools from me. Like, I had that cool—"

"Stay focused," Matthew interrupted, starting the car.

The watch buzzed with a message from Sarah. "Looks like the Jeep is headed north and just went straight through the intersection up ahead," I told Matthew.

Matthew nodded and turned right out of the parking lot. We caught up to the Jeep a few minutes later and followed a few paces behind as he made several random turns.

"It doesn't seem like he's headed to the capitol or back to MAX," Matthew noted as we took another turn.

"Maybe he knows he's being followed," I suggested. A wild idea popped into my head. "Hey! What if—"

"Nope," Matthew interrupted.

"You haven't even heard my idea."

"It's probably ridiculous."

I rolled my eyes. "You're going to hear it anyways. What if I jump into the bed of the truck and hide, then you'll pull up next to the Jeep and I'll jump inside. That way I can hopefully stop the Jeep and we'll get the chip and Agent Holton." The more I thought about it, the more fun the idea sounded.

"That sounds ridiculous." Matthew's far-too-practical brain was the party pooper to most of my good ideas.

I crossed my arms. "Fine. Tell me when you have a better idea."

We made two more turns in silence.

I glanced at Matthew. "Well?"

He huffed. "We don't have time to think up anything better."

"Yes!" I did a fist-pump and unbuckled my seatbelt. Before Matthew could change his mind, I hit the open window button for the back window and crawled out into the bed of the truck.

"Luke, you don't even have any coms! How are we going to stay in contact?" Matthew called.

I shrugged. "Hand signals, I guess." I crouched in the bed of the truck and waited for Matthew to pull up alongside the Jeep. I steadied myself as the truck sped up and moved into the other lane. Matthew raised his hand and pointed three times at the Jeep. Starting from the opposite side of the truck bed, I took what little of a running start I could and jumped. I grabbed the crossbar on the driver's side of the Jeep and held on, now awkwardly face to face with Agent Holton.

"Sup." I grinned.

"Luke Mason?" He looked surprised and angry. With a jerk he swiftly turned right down an empty neighborhood street. I fought to hold on through the turn. Once the Jeep straightened out, I pulled myself up on top of the frame. Holton swerved back and forth down the street, then slammed on his brakes, flipping me forward onto the hood of the car. I pulled myself back over the windshield and dropped onto the console between the driver and passenger seats.

"Let's pull the car over, Holton." I pushed myself into Holton's space, fighting for a hand on the wheel. I jerked the wheel to the right and pulled the parking brake on. We screeched to a stop in the middle of the street.

Matthew stopped his truck right next to the Jeep. "Get out of the car slowly."

Holton started reaching for the floor of the Jeep, so I beat him to it. A pistol holster was underneath the edge of the driver's chair. I pulled the pistol out and held it to Holton's back. "Just get out of the car, dude." *I seriously hope no one is home watching us through their windows.*

Holton slowly pulled the door handle and stepped out of

the Jeep. Matthew jumped out of the truck and stood in front of Holton, dwarfing the agent. "Where's the chip?"

"You're going to be in trouble with the feds for holding up an FBI agent," Holton retorted.

Matthew was unphased. "So are you for stealing classified evidence. Now hand it over."

Holton pulled the chip from his pocket and tossed it on the ground. As Matthew bent down to grab it, Holton stomped on the chip, grinding his heel.

Matthew let out a low growl as he picked up the crushed chip. "Get in the truck." Matthew grabbed a pair of handcuffs from his glovebox and handcuffed Holton to the interior car handle by the passenger seat. Once he was secure, Matthew turned to me, handing me his suit jacket with my wig inside. "You drive the Jeep back to HQ. I'll straighten everything out with Agent Brandon and let him know you have the Jeep."

I nodded. "Thanks, dude."

Matthew gave me a fist bump. "No problem."

"You're back!" Daniel exclaimed as he opened the hotel door.

I nodded as I walked in the door and plopped down in a dining room chair. I filled the two in on everything that happened with the FBI, Matthew's rescue, and catching Holton. "This has been quite the day. I'm going to need new coms."

Sarah nodded and tapped a gray container on the table. "We've got those ready for tomorrow."

Daniel took a seat beside me. "Do you think Holton got word to MAX that you've been undercover?"

I sighed. "I have no clue. Unless Matthew can find out that information, I don't think I'll know till I go back."

"Well, at least now that Liam and the two chips are confiscated, there should be enough evidence to convict MAX. And we can focus on getting Rebecca and Isaac out," Daniel said.

Sarah frowned. "It'll be much harder to get Rebecca and Isaac out of there if Holton got the word to MAX about you working undercover."

I nodded, running a hand through my already wild hair. *Lord, please keep the word from getting to MAX. I need to stay undercover. Rebecca needs me to stay undercover. Lord, help us.*

"Where is Liam?" MAX went straight to the obvious. He leaned his crossed arms against his ornate wooden desk, his face dark. Matthew wasn't able to get Holton to say whether he'd gotten word to MAX about my undercover role as Jack, but since MAX was focused on Liam's absence, I guessed MAX didn't know.

"He was apprehended," I replied coolly.

"And the mission? If Liam was apprehended—"

"My chip was taken care of, but Liam was caught placing his. Considering what a blabbermouth he is, it is likely that my chip was also discovered." I crossed my arms, shaking my head.

MAX tapped his fingers impatiently on the desk. "This isn't like you, Jack."

"You know I prefer to work alone." *At least he still thinks I'm Jack.*

"But if you suspected Liam's incompetence, then you should've had him stay in the getaway car and done all the work yourself!" MAX said, his voice rising.

"Liam has been a ball and chain since I returned from my last mission," I said with a shrug.

MAX's eyes narrowed. "And you just added more steps to my plan, steps that were unnecessary had you done this mission properly." He growled. "This was not your best work."

"Understood."

MAX leaned back in his chair and sighed. "Rebecca could probably get me into the government programs I need access to, but she's being quite stubborn. I don't know that she would do any hacking without putting up quite a fight."

I nodded. *That's an understatement.*

"I may need you to make her talk. I've waited long enough for those codes, and too long to manually orchestrate the power outage. I need the codes, and I need her to do some hacking for me."

I nodded again. "That can be arranged."

A knock sounded on the office door. MAX straightened in his chair. "Come in."

The door swung open, and two guards walked in with Rebecca between them, pushing her toward MAX's desk. I tried to keep my face neutral. Seeing her handcuffed and pushed around by the tight grips of these two guards made me angry. *Lord, help me. I can't blow this.*

"Surely you've figured out why you're here by now," MAX said, his tone exasperated.

Rebecca, per usual, rolled her eyes. "Not really." Her voice was more sarcastic than the eyeroll.

MAX slapped his desk. "I will play no more games! I have waited you out, but enough is enough. We will get those codes from you one way or another—I promise you that." MAX stood and walked around to the other side of his desk, standing face-to-face with Rebecca. "I can make your life and the life of your brother miserable until you talk."

Rebecca stared unflinchingly. "I'd like to see you try."

Rebecca, that's a foolish thing to say! I thought. I took a deep breath in hopes of controlling my face from growing red.

"Besides," she continued, "you've yet to prove to me that my brother is even here."

"And yet you came all this way to save him. How do you not believe he is here?" MAX challenged.

"The longer you've taken to prove he's here, the more I've begun to doubt it."

The two stared at each other for a minute, a standoff between a man who always gets his way and my girlfriend, the most stubborn agent I'd ever met. Slowly, MAX raised his hand and snapped at one of the guards. "Bring in Isaac."

The guard nodded and hurried from the room. Moments later he came back through the door, yanking a young man through the door. He looked just like his sisters—dark haired, blue-eyed, pale skin, and towering above the guard next to him. He looked tired, his clothes rumpled, and he had a bruise on his angular jaw.

Rebecca turned to see her brother. Her challenging expression melted. "Isaac," she whispered. She bit her lip, her eyebrows scrunched and her eyes glistening.

Isaac managed a small smile. "Hi, sis."

MAX yanked Rebecca back around to face him. I tensed, ready to punch him in the face, but I restrained myself. *Why do I have to be Jack right now?*

"You have your proof. Now, the codes?"

Rebecca swallowed hard, averting her gaze. Slowly, she tilted her chin up and stared at MAX defiantly. "No."

MAX grunted. "Well, if you choose the hard path, that's your prerogative. Trust me, once Jack is through with you, you'll wish you had changed your tune." MAX turned to the guards and waved them out. Just as they reached the door, a knock sounded, and it swung open. Two more guards entered, dragging in a very angry man in his thirties—a man about my size with curly blonde hair. I watched the color drain from Rebecca's face as she watched the guards pull the man to face MAX.

"Sir, this man entered the premises claiming to be Jack and never showed his ID," the guard began.

My eyes met Jack's. I could see the resemblance in all ways but one—his eyes flamed with hate.

I believe this means I am now dead meat.

CHAPTER 12

"Jack?" MAX glanced between the two of us, looking both confused and surprised. His expression slowly changed to recognition, and I knew my cheap wig wasn't cutting it.

"Who are you?" Jack demanded.

Yeah, he's definitely more of a baritone than my tenor, I thought, glancing between Jack and MAX. *Maybe if I don't say anything, MAX won't notice.*

Daniel's voice boomed in my coms. "Get out now."

How? I knew I could book it while everyone stood around in shock, but I couldn't leave Isaac and Rebecca to face the real Jack. *Lord, I need help fast.*

There were six guards in the room now, but every guard held onto a prisoner. They still looked confused, so it was time to make my exit. I bolted for the door.

"Let Jack go!" MAX screamed.

I ran down the hall, MAX's screamed orders floating to my ears as he told the guards to put Rebecca and Isaac back in their rooms and then to find the imposter—me.

I pressed the button for the elevator and the doors opened immediately. I stepped inside and turned around. Two guards were running my direction. I hit the close door button and the third floor. The elevator started moving. I jumped onto the metal handrail, bracing myself against the corner of the elevator, and pushed open the hatch for the top of the elevator. The elevator dinged, signaling its arrival at the third floor.

I should've picked a higher floor. I grasped the edge of the hatch, swung myself beneath, and pulled myself up as the door opened. I quickly shut the hatch and prayed no one saw me. *Now to wait.*

The elevator stayed put for a minute, then began descending. I counted the floors as I passed, noting that it returned to the second basement.

"Why are you still in the building?" Daniel asked.

I rolled my eyes. "Because I'm not leaving without Isaac and Rebecca."

"If you get caught, you're dead. And you won't be able to help us if you're dead."

"I'll just avoid getting caught," I replied, bracing as the elevator began moving up again. It made a stop at the first level, then continued up again. We passed door after door, until we reached the top, the twelfth floor. *So, is this where they've been holding Rebecca and Isaac?*

I opened the hatch a crack and peered down. Sure enough, four guards led Rebecca and Isaac out of the elevator. Once they were all out of the elevator, I slowly opened the hatch all the way. I held onto the edge and slid down, hanging on for a second before dropping to the ground as softly as I could. Two guards led Rebecca into a room at the end of the hall. Two more guards were two doors from the elevator, pushing Isaac inside through the open door. No one looked my direction. I pulled my stun gun from its concealed holster and ran at the guards leading Isaac. I fired a shot at each guard before they could react. They both fell to the ground and Isaac turned around to stare at me, confused and scared.

"I'm Luke with Truth Squad," I said, knowing I still looked like Jack. I grabbed some keys off the belt of one of the guards and unlocked Isaac's handcuffs. I grabbed Isaac's hand and pulled him out of the room.

"Hey!" A guard stepped out of Rebecca's prison room and stared wide-eyed at us.

"Let's go." I pulled on Isaac's arm and ran, half-dragging him, to the elevator. I swallowed hard as I closed the elevator doors, realizing I couldn't go back for Rebecca. Isaac was obviously too weak, and we had no time. *I can't do this!* my mind screamed as the elevator rushed down flight after flight, farther and farther away from Rebecca. *How could you be this close to rescuing her and fail?* I gritted my teeth and prayed, *Lord, please keep her safe.* The elevator door dinged and slid open at the first floor. *Because right now I can't.*

"Luke, go through the courtyard and exit through the storefront. I have the getaway car waiting for you," Daniel spoke into my coms.

"Got it." I tugged on Isaac's arm. "I know you don't feel like it, but you've got to run if we want out of here alive."

Isaac nodded and hurried with me through the busy first floor. Most people didn't bat an eye as we hurried past, so I figured word hadn't spread too much about the Jack imposter. Or Isaac's escape.

Isaac's breathing was becoming labored, and he looked pale, so I slowed my pace a little. I could see the door to the courtyard now. "We're almost there," I said, looking over my shoulder at Isaac. "You've got this."

I turned back around and whammed into my double. Jack looked surprised, then his eyes narrowed. "Found him!"

Without thinking, my reflexes took over and I socked him in the stomach. I pulled his arm and shoved him behind us, then took off running, dragging Isaac along behind me. There wasn't time to be slow anymore. I could hear Jack calling for guards to come after us. We reached the door and I pulled it open, shoving Isaac through before following him.

"Keep going," I said. I heard the door open and close behind us.

Suddenly, someone grabbed Isaac's arm. I turned to free Isaac, but I saw the familiar face of my best friend. Daniel nodded at me. With two of us to support Isaac, we picked up the pace and made it to the storefront. I glanced behind and saw two guards tailing us the entire way through the store.

We hurried out the giant front doors and got Isaac into the car before driving off. The guards didn't come after our car, but they watched us leave.

"We'll have to ditch the getaway car," I said as we pulled out.

Daniel nodded. "Mr. Truth expected as much. Matthew is waiting for us down the street."

"Good," I said, my mind half distracted by the fact that every mile we drove took us farther from Rebecca. *Lord, protect her.*

"Yup." Daniel glanced in the rearview mirror at Isaac. "I think we need to head to urgent care. I'll have Matthew meet us there."

I looked back to see Isaac resting his head in his hands, his skin very pale. "I agree."

"I'm fine," Isaac moaned, his voice weak and dry. "I just need water, that's all."

"Well, we'd better play it safe," Daniel replied, pressing a button on his watch. "Matthew, we're headed to urgent care with Isaac."

"You need to get Rebecca out of there," Isaac said, his voice trailing off into a cough. "Now that I'm gone," he coughed again, "they can't threaten me, and she's so stubborn—" his voice trailed off and he shook his head, leaning back with his eyes closed. "Why did I ever take this job?"

It took a couple hours to get back to our hotel room. After Isaac was admitted to urgent care, Matthew showed up to drop Sarah off to stay with Isaac. Then, Daniel and I drove to a random area in downtown and left the getaway car along with my curly-blonde wig. We walked a few blocks, and then Matthew picked us up and drove us back to the hotel.

On the drive to urgent care, Isaac had explained a little about how he ended up with MAX. He was a computer hacker, a very good one, just like his sister. He'd been okay with shady deals here and there since it made good money. When MAX hired him, he thought he was just doing a couple deals scoping out competing political candidates, but MAX paid so well he just kept working with him. Eventually, MAX asked Isaac to crack the codes Zaiden had given to Rebecca. He'd tried and tried but couldn't do it. MAX was getting fed up with Isaac, and the more Isaac saw of MAX's plans, the more he wanted out. One day he decided to quit, but MAX wouldn't let him quit—he knew too much. Since then, he'd been a pawn to get Rebecca to D.C.

Mr. Truth and Agent Brandon were waiting for us back at our hotel room. "Glad you made it back," Mr. Truth said with a smile as I walked in. I could tell from the look on his face he had been worried I wasn't going to.

I tried to smile back, but I figured he could tell it was fake. "Thanks."

He gave me a knowing look. "Well, let's get down to business."

Agent Brandon cleared his throat. "Through apprehending Liam and the data we gathered from the one good computer chip Holton didn't destroy, we have enough evidence to take down MAX's entire operation. Liam gave good testimony to all of MAX's plans in exchange for a lighter sentence."

Mr. Truth folded his arms. "We've got to make sure Rebecca is safe before we take down MAX."

Agent Brandon cleared his throat. "The FBI is leaving that to your jurisdiction, Mr. Truth. However, the longer we wait, the harder it will be to stop this operation before it's too late." He glanced at me apologetically. "Our leadership has decided that you have thirty-six hours to complete a rescue operation before we move in."

My jaw dropped, but Mr. Truth quickly put a hand on my shoulder. "Understood."

I clamped my jaw shut and nodded, swallowing hard to hold back the emotions building up in my throat. "So, what's the plan?" *And how are we doing this in thirty-six hours?*

Matthew stepped forward. "I think I have an idea. Daniel, can you pull up the floor plans for the building?"

Daniel took a seat at the computer and began typing. "Here it is," he said, turning the laptop for everyone to see.

"Luke, where is Rebecca being held?" Matthew asked.

"The twelfth floor."

"And where is MAX's office?"

"The second basement."

"So, here's the idea. We need to rescue Rebecca, but we also need to let America know what's really going on with MAX. I mean, he seems like a great guy to a lot of Americans who are planning to vote for him. But everyone needs to know the truth before the FBI jumps in on this case," Matthew explained.

Daniel nodded. "Otherwise, it will look like the government is interfering with elections in a way they never should."

"Exactly." Matthew pointed to the basement. "So, I think we should send Daniel and Sarah here to get video evidence of MAX's true character out to the public. While they work on that, Luke and I will go here," he pointed to the top floor, "and rescue Rebecca. Once we've exited the building, the FBI can take over and shut down the operation."

Mr. Truth tilted his head thoughtfully. "It seems risky to have you all split up like that. You'll be so far apart, you can't provide backup for one another."

"I know we're leaving this in your jurisdiction, so you have the final say," Agent Brandon jumped in, "but I do think Matthew has a good point about getting video evidence out to the public. And we'll be ready to go once the thirty-six hours are up, so we can provide backup at that point." He glanced at his watch. "I've got to be going, but fill me in on the plan before it takes effect."

"Will do," Mr. Truth said, shaking his friend's hand. Agent Brandon hurried out, and the rest of us took a seat around the table.

We sat silently for a few minutes, Matthew tapping his foot impatiently, Daniel studying the map of the building, and Mr. Truth resting his chin on folded hands with eyes closed. One of his many admirable traits—he was a man of prayer. I closed my eyes and rubbed my hands over my face. *Lord, please give wisdom to all of us, and to the FBI, as we make our plans. Thwart the work of the enemy. And help us to rescue Rebecca and stop MAX before it's too late.*

"I'll take care of communications and tracking." I opened my eyes and met Mr. Truth's commanding gaze. "I'll call in a few of our men who're stationed in Virginia; they'll be here in time to be backup in case they're needed."

Excitement blazed in Matthew's eyes. "So, we have a plan?"

Mr. Truth smiled. "I believe we do."

It was midnight by the time we'd finished strategizing our plan, backup plan, and necessary equipment. Our plan seemed solid, but I couldn't shake the nagging question in the back of my head—*what if we're too late? What if we can't save Rebecca?*

Matthew had headed to his own hotel room down the hall and Daniel had gone to bed. I sat on the couch staring out the window, waiting for Mr. Truth to head out. He was finishing his third cup of black, decaf coffee.

Mr. Truth walked over and sat down next to me, letting out a long, slow breath. I knew that meant he was preparing himself for a long discussion. Mr. Truth was kind of like my dad, in that way. My parents had done overseas missions through Truth Squad and died in a terrorist attack. I'd grown up with my grandparents who'd sent me to Truth Academy as a kid, per my parents' request. But my grandparents were skeptical when I showed interest in becoming a Truth Squad agent like my parents. They warned me I was taking this "defending-the-truth" stuff too far, just like my own parents did, and it had gotten them killed. My grandparents said they didn't want to be "too extreme about Jesus," especially not after losing their son and daughter-in-law. So, over the years, I'd often turned to Mr. Truth for guidance and answers to my many questions.

"What's bothering you?" Mr. Truth asked, taking a sip of coffee.

I gave a half smile. "You can't read my mind?"

He smiled and shook his head. "No, but I can tell you're struggling. This whole mission seems to be weighing on you more than normal."

I nodded, trying to pause and think before I spouted off an answer.

"Is it Rebecca?" Mr. Truth asked. "Is your relationship complicating the mission?"

I felt my face grow red as I shrugged. "Kind of. But I think... maybe it's deeper than that. I mean, I am worried about her safety, and I feel like I should be protecting her somehow."

"But you also know the risks that both of you signed up for as Truth Squad agents, right?" Mr. Truth smiled knowingly, and I nodded. "You know I understand this very well, don't you? Mary and I have served as Truth Squad agents for over twenty years together. It's not easy to go on missions and keep a level head when you're serving alongside your bride."

"But Mary tends to monitor missions from the base. She doesn't go out into the field," I said, sounding more agitated than I meant to.

Mr. Truth raised his eyebrows. "Luke, before we had Jonathan, and before I became president of Truth Squad, we both did special operations. Granted, Mary never resigned from Truth Squad to track down a mob boss, so I can't relate on that level, but I have experienced the tension of work and relationships."

I sighed. "Sorry, I didn't mean to sound that way. It's just," I paused, not sure what I was going to say. "It's just... is it worth it?"

"What do you mean?"

"Like, I have the ring, I was going to propose. But should I? Is it worth getting married if it's going to interfere with my work so much?" I rubbed my forehead.

Mr. Truth laughed and clasped my shoulder. "Luke, you would be miserable if you didn't ask Rebecca to marry you and kept on working together." He paused. "Or are you thinking of quitting Truth Squad?"

"No way!" I shook my head. "I believe in what Truth Squad is doing. It's just... I don't know, something deeper." I ran my fingers through my hair, trying to figure it out. "It's something about this mission in particular. Like, the stakes are so high. This plot is way bigger than we expected. What if we don't win?"

"Hmm." Mr. Truth nodded, a spark of understanding flashing into his eyes. "You're worried about what will happen if we fail? If MAX succeeds in his uprising? What will happen to Truth Squad, to you and Rebecca, to our country?"

I nodded. "There's so much evil in this plot. Why couldn't we have known about it and stopped it sooner? Why aren't more people standing up to this?"

"Are you asking what God's up to, why He doesn't seem to be doing anything?"

Mr. Truth's question hurt, but I knew he was right. *Am I a doubting Thomas?* I wondered, half-sarcastically and half-genuinely.

Mr. Truth rubbed his chin thoughtfully. "There's so much more going on that we can't see. We see the human side of things, but there is a deeper, spiritual battle happening right now. There always is. And God is always moving, even when we don't see it. Remember that story about Elisha and his servant?"

I nodded. "The king of Aram sent an army to capture Elisha, and the servant freaked out when he saw the army coming. But Elisha told him that they had more people on their side than the army did, which sounded ridiculous because it was just Elisha and his servant there," I said, getting excited as I recounted the story. "So, Elisha prayed for his servant's eyes to be opened, and God opened his eyes to see the mountains full of horses and chariots of fire, and God won the battle without a fight."

"And in the book of Daniel, an angel told Daniel about a battle he'd been fighting that kept him from coming to Daniel right away," Mr. Truth said.

I grinned. "And Ephesians says to wear the armor of God because our battle is really spiritual."

Mr. Truth nodded. "Truth Squad's goal is to defend the truth, and now more than ever it needs done. Defending the truth isn't just a cool motto; it's a spiritual battle. The devil doesn't want Christians standing up for the truth and spreading the gospel, and he will do what he can to stop us." Mr. Truth paused and sipped his coffee. "We tend to long for the easy, 'white-picket-fence' life, but if we're not experiencing trials, then are we really standing up for the truth?"

"You're referring to 2 Timothy 3:12, 'Indeed, all who desire to live godly in Christ Jesus will be persecuted'?" I asked. Mr. Truth nodded, and I sighed. "I know this stuff, but it's hard to really know it in my heart, you know? It's hard to hear more people criticizing Truth Squad, saying we're going too far, and spreading lies about us, and it's hard to feel like we're the only ones standing up for what's right."

"We're not the only ones standing up for the truth," Mr. Truth replied. "There's Christians all over the world standing up for the gospel, many of whom are experiencing persecution for doing so. That's one reason Truth Squad fights to defend the truth not just in America but internationally."

I nodded. "But what if we lose and MAX wins? What if he shuts down Truth Squad?" I lowered my voice, "What if we start experiencing real persecution here in America?" I felt my face flush as I voiced what I was embarrassed to admit. *God, I confess that thought scares me,* I prayed silently.

"Then we trust God to give us the strength to keep standing even then," Mr. Truth replied solemnly. "We trust Him to help us keep being the light of the world, to keep sharing Christ and His peace, joy, love, and truth with those around us. The gospel mission doesn't change, no matter what happens in this world." Mr. Truth took a deep breath. "Luke, I've wondered about this myself. As the president of Truth Squad, I've worried about what would happen if we were shut down, worried about it more than I should have. I've worried about what the future might hold for my son. I've worried about a lot of different things, but God's Word says to pray instead of worrying, and God promises that He will be with us no matter what we walk through. That is what I cling to." He smiled. "I clung to that back as a young agent serving alongside my wife as newlyweds, and I cling to it today, right now as we face this mission."

I leaned back against the couch and let Mr. Truth's words sink in. "Thanks. I needed to hear that."

Mr. Truth placed his hand on my shoulder. "Let's pray."

CHAPTER 13

I slid my bullet-proof vest on and tightened the straps.

"You okay?"

I jumped, glancing up at Matthew.

He nodded, a small grin tugging at the corner of his mouth. "You've been extremely slow putting your gear on."

I paused, not wanting to talk. I knew it would ease the tension I was feeling, but I didn't know what to say. I opened my mouth but couldn't think up any good excuses. I went back to tightening the straps on my vest.

"It's tough," Matthew said, walking over to me and clapping a hand on my shoulder. "Any rescue operation for one of our agents is tough enough, but throw in the girl you like?" He shook his head. "That takes it to another level."

I nodded. "That's exactly right."

Daniel and Mr. Truth walked into the room. Mr. Truth cleared his throat. "Luke, if you need me to send another guy in for you—"

"No." I shook my head. "I know the ins and outs of that building from being undercover. And I—" I paused and took a deep breath. "I want to be there for Rebecca, too."

Mr. Truth smiled wistfully. "I'll admit, I understand that feeling. I had to rescue Mary a time or two when we were younger." His eyes watered and he stopped.

Sarah walked into the room all geared up, but her face looked as worried as I felt. Daniel hurried over to her and grasped her hand, smiling reassuringly. She smiled back, the worry easing from her face.

"Coms check," Mr. Truth said.

We worked through each piece of equipment, making sure everything was ready to go. "Alright, I think we're ready. Let's pray before you head out," Mr. Truth said. We bowed our heads, and he began, "Lord, thank You for another day of life to serve You. We ask You to clear the way before us. Keep us safe, give us clear minds, and may Your righteousness prevail today. In Jesus' name, Amen."

"Amen," we echoed.

Matthew straightened, his commanding game-face on. "Let's go."

We headed outside to our vehicle. We were leaving at five o'clock in the morning, so it was still dark out. I hadn't slept much the night before, but with the amount of adrenaline I was feeling, I was sure I wouldn't notice until the mission was over.

We drove out behind the JX headquarters and parked out of sight from the building. The loading dock for the trucks seemed to be the best way for us to get in undetected. I led the way through the darkness to the loading docks. A truck was just pulling away from a dock when we arrived. Matthew hoisted himself up onto the dock and held the bay door open. The rest of us pulled ourselves up onto the dock and hurried inside, then Matthew quietly closed the door.

"Let's go," I whispered, staying along the shadowy walls as we hurried to a door in the far-right corner. I pushed open the door for the others to walk through to the courtyard.

The courtyard was completely dark and empty; no one was here to start up any of the shops yet. We hurried through without worrying about staying in the shadows since we had our camera blocking devices. We used a magnetic lock disabler to get through the badge scanner and into MAX's headquarters on the other side of the courtyard. I stepped through the door and saw a lone guard with his back to us. Before he could see us, I tased him and Matthew and Daniel dragged him out into the courtyard.

We hurried to the elevator, and Matthew and I stepped inside. "Okay, once the elevator has gone up to the eighth floor, you can open these doors and climb down the shaft to the second basement," Matthew reminded Daniel and Sarah. Since we didn't know the codes to reach the basements or the top four floors, climbing the elevator shaft was our best option. "Keep in touch. Let's be in and out as fast as we can."

Daniel nodded. "Got it."

I hit the eighth-floor button and the doors slid shut. After what felt like watching two snails race across a stump, the elevator finally came to a stop at the eighth floor. Matthew opened the hatch to the elevator, and we climbed out. We each wore special climbing gloves to help us get up the metal walls to the top floor. The gloves had two buttons, one button suctioned the glove to the wall, the other released it from the wall so you could keep climbing.

I suctioned the gloves to the wall just above my head and pulled myself up, using my legs to brace against the wall. Matthew started climbing next to me. It felt like trying to run underwater as we slowly climbed the wall.

"We're in the basement," Daniel said through our coms.

"Got it," Matthew replied, grunting as he pulled himself higher up the wall.

We were halfway up the shaft when we heard the elevator rumble to life. I looked down to see the elevator coming toward us. "We might have trouble."

Matthew glanced down. "Well, if it gets to us, we'll just release our grips and ride it up."

We watched, tense, as the elevator continued upward. "Okay, I think we'll need to release in three, two, one." I pressed both release buttons on my gloves and dropped onto the elevator, bending my knees to soften the sound as I landed. Matthew landed beside me. The elevator went up to the eleventh floor and stopped. "Hey, it did part of the work for us!" I said, grinning.

Matthew nodded. "Let's keep going."

We continued our slow climb up the wall. Eventually, the elevator rumbled again and made its descent. I paused to watch the elevator go down and down and down. "It might be going all the way to the basement."

Matthew shook his head. "That's not good."

We finally reached the twelfth-floor doors. After bracing our feet and securing one hand in place, we each grabbed one side of the door and pulled it open. The hallway was dark and there were no guards. We pulled ourselves inside and slowly made our way down the hall.

"Weird there are no guards out," Matthew muttered.

I nodded. "Rebecca was in the room at the end of the hall."

We hurried to the door. The lock was a combination lock. I grabbed a lock pick decoder from my belt and placed it over the door. I listened to the metal bolts tumbling inside the door, then a click. I turned the knob and pushed the door open. The room was dark.

"Hello?" I whispered.

Matthew pulled a flashlight off his belt and flashed it around the room. It was empty. "Are you sure she was in this room?"

"Yes," I said, my heartrate picking up. "But maybe they moved rooms. Let's check the other doors."

We unlocked every door in the hall. Every room was empty. I was starting to feel panicked now. "Where could she be? What if—"

I couldn't finish my paranoid thoughts because our coms were filled with commotion.

"Daniel, what's going on?" I asked. Loud banging and yelling voices filled my earpiece.

Matthew glanced at me. "If my suspicions are right, they probably got caught."

"Let's hope your suspicions are wrong," I said, hurrying back to the elevator shaft.

A few seconds later, Sarah whispered, "Uh, Daniel just got captured."

I glanced back at Matthew. He closed his eyes and shook his head. "Stay low," he warned.

"Hey!" Sarah's voice rang in my ear.

"Oh, no," I said running a hand through my hair.

"Oh no is right." Matthew shook his head. "Now we've got three agents to rescue."

"I guess we're headed down to the basement," I said, looking down the elevator shaft. "Too bad we can't hitch a ride right now."

Matthew sat down, grabbed onto the ledge, and lowered himself into the shaft, then stuck his gloves to the wall. I followed suit and made my way swinging down the shaft. It was much faster climbing down than up. I felt like we needed superhero theme music climbing down the shaft, and pretty soon I found myself humming the most epic theme I could make up right then.

"Luke, be quiet," Matthew hissed.

"I'm not being that loud. Besides, who's going to hear us from inside this metal box? It's not like MAX agents have bat ears or anything," I joked.

Matthew glared at me. "Focus on the mission."

I nodded and kept my tune to myself. For a few minutes. Slowly my theme song made its way back to my vocal cords.

"Luke, stop humming," Matthew growled.

I sighed. "I can't help it! And tell me again who can hear us?"

Just then, the elevator doors several floors above us opened. "They can!" Matthew muttered as we plastered ourselves as close to the wall as possible.

My eyes were wide. "Why didn't the elevator go up when they opened the doors?" I whispered.

"They must've known Daniel and Sarah got down this way and shut down the elevator," Matthew muttered. A flashlight shown down the shaft, scanning the walls. "They're going to see us. We have to keep moving."

I began swinging my arms, scurrying down the wall as fast as possible, getting back into a rhythm of sticking one glove while unsticking another. The flashlight finally reached us for a moment as we hurried down the walls.

"I see an intruder, possibly two," the guard's voice reverberated down the shaft to our ears.

"Just keep going," Matthew muttered.

"There'll be guys waiting for us at the bottom," I said.

"We'll be ready for them."

We finished our descent and dropped onto the elevator that still sat on the bottom floor. I slowly opened the hatch and Matthew peered inside, his taser ready. The elevator doors were still closed.

"I'll cover you while you drop down, then I'll follow," Matthew said. "Be careful, though. This seems fishy."

"What fish?" I joked, jumping down the hatch. The doors stayed closed, and the elevator stayed put. Matthew jumped down behind me. "We each pull one door open and be prepared for whatever's on the other side?"

Matthew nodded and took his position. "On three." He held up three fingers. *Three. Two. One.* I jerked my door toward me and ducked back behind the elevator wall for cover. A bullet whizzed past and hit the back wall. I peered out and saw two guards facing us. Matthew shot one with his taser, and I got the second.

"There's got to be more," I whispered. The hallway was completely empty. We pulled the two guards into the elevator and zip-tied their wrists and ankles before cautiously walking down the hall.

"I'll cover you while you check the doors on the left, and you do the same for me," Matthew muttered, taser in hand.

I nodded and grasped the knob of the first door. I gave a quick countdown with my fingers, then pushed the door open. The room was completely empty. Matthew checked the door on his side of the hall. Also empty.

I pushed open the second door. Before I could duck out of the way, I was tackled. My back slammed the floor and the wind rushed from my lungs. The guard who jumped me was a mammoth. I fought like a beached whale to take in some air while wrestling to get free from this guy. The guard shoved me onto my stomach and handcuffed me. I continued making squawking noises as I tried to breathe, watching as Matthew fought another guard who was of smaller stature than the mammoth sitting on my back. Finally, a gulp of air made it to my lungs, allowing me to start squirming again under my captor.

"I could use some help," I grunted.

Matthew sent a knock-out blow to the other guard's chin and pulled a small dart from his belt, stabbing the larger man's arm. The guard stood up and threw a punch at Matthew, who reflexively raised his arms to block.

Now that I was no longer pinned, I rolled over and swung my leg to trip the guard. The tranquilizer dart Matthew hit him with was already taking effect, so he toppled easily and was soon out of it.

"Can you uncuff me?" I asked, still lying on the ground.

Matthew found the keys on the guard's belt and removed my handcuffs, then gave me a hand. I jumped to my feet. "Well, that's four down. However many more to go!"

I opened the third door on my side of the hall. Empty. Matthew swung open the door on his side. A bullet whizzed past and hit the opposite wall. We ducked behind the wall as two more bullets flew past.

"I think I saw four guards around Daniel and Sarah," Matthew said. "Cover me."

Matthew darted into the room. I stood just outside the doorway and hit the nearest guard with my taser before following Matthew into the room. We took cover behind a large desk. Matthew tased a second guard. I peered out from our hiding spot. Daniel and Sarah were sitting in metal chairs back-to-back, tied up. A guard stood on either side, and the two guards we'd tased lay on the floor. Daniel swung his legs and knocked over the guard beside him.

"Now," I said, jumping up and rushing forward. Matthew tased the guard next to Sarah, while I jumped on the guard

Daniel knocked over. I needed answers to some questions. I zip-tied his wrists and ankles, then flipped him over to look him in the eyes. "Tell me where Rebecca and Jack are."

The guard kept his mouth shut. He was obviously not intimidated, or maybe the thought of snitching on Jack was scarier than me with a taser.

Matthew came over and nudged me off the guard. He picked the guard up from the floor and slammed him into the chair Daniel was no longer sitting in. "You tell us right now where Rebecca and Jack are."

The guard's eyes were wide now. Matthew didn't need to make any threats. His size and muscles did it for him. I noticed Matthew had also picked up a gun from one of the tased guards, which probably helped the intimidation factor.

I turned to Daniel and Sarah while Matthew continued his interrogation. "You guys okay?"

Sarah nodded. "We need to find my sister."

"She's not down here," Daniel said. I handed him some zip-ties and we started tying up the guards. "MAX's office was a trap, obviously. There was nothing but a room full of guards waiting for us. He must've guessed you'd be back for Rebecca."

"Rebecca wasn't upstairs like before," I said.

Mr. Truth's voice buzzed in my ear. "We just received word that power outages have occurred in Spokane, Olympia, Portland, Salem, San Diego, Los Angeles, San Fransisco, Sacramento, and Las Vegas in the last ten minutes."

Sarah's eyes widened and her face grew pale. "We need to hurry. If MAX has already gotten started—" her voice trailed off.

Matthew joined us. "The guard doesn't know where Rebecca is. He just knows they moved her because they were sure Luke was coming back. But he does know that MAX's control room for the synchronized power outage is in the first basement. I'm betting we'll find Rebecca there."

"Let's go." I took off down the hall.

"Slow down, dude," Daniel called, running up and grabbing my shoulder. "We've got to stick together. Rushing in is going to cause more danger."

I swallowed and nodded, slowing my pace to stick with the group. We climbed back up the elevator shaft to the first basement and opened the doors. The hall was full of guards. I grabbed a smoke bomb from my belt, pulled the fuse, and tossed it into the hall. I put on some special sunglasses made for vision in smokey areas and then hoisted myself through the door into the hall. Matthew put his special smoke glasses on and began taking care of the guards in the hall. Daniel, Sarah, and I began checking the doors. The first two rooms were full of tech equipment. Daniel opened the third door, and a guard spun around in surprise, knocking Daniel over with a baton in his hand. My heart skipped a beat when I saw behind the guard into the room—Jack staring surprised and angry at the open doorway, and Rebecca tied up in a chair, a look of relief on her worn, bruised face.

Sarah and I rushed in. My blood was past boiling—it was spontaneously combusting. I charged Jack and knocked him flat on his back. I was ready to punch his face, but Jack was ready for me and suddenly I found myself on my back and blocking a punch to my own face. Jack's look was pure hatred. *I think he's still mad I faked being him.* After blocking a few blows, I rolled out from underneath him. I jumped up and whirled to face Jack—and got an uppercut. So I was on my back again. I blinked hard to clear the stars from my vision. Jack was back on me, and he pulled a knife from his belt. *Why does the equation of me and Jack in the same room always end in dead meat?*

"Hey!" Sarah's scream startled both Jack and me. We both turned just as Sarah slammed a metal chair against the back of Jack's head. I caught Jack from falling on me with the knife as he blacked out. I pushed him off and got up, hurrying over to Rebecca.

I knelt beside her chair. "You okay?" I asked, my voice choaking slightly.

She smiled. "Now I am."

I grinned and picked up Jack's knife. "You'll probably be even better when you're not tied up." The moment I finished cutting the ropes and put the knife down, Rebecca jumped up and hugged me. I smiled and wrapped my arms around her, not ever wanting to let go again.

Sarah jumped into the hug, whispering in Rebecca's ear, "I'm so glad you're okay."

A fake cough came from the doorway. I snapped back to the mission, turning to see Daniel and Matthew in the doorway, most of the smoke cleared from the hall. I slowly let go of Rebecca and smiled. "Let's go!"

As we walked over to join Daniel and Matthew, I noticed Rebecca's steps falter a bit. *She needs to get out of here, and she's definitely not going to admit that.*

"Rebecca, where will we find MAX?" Matthew asked.

"He's planned the mass power outage for today. He should be in the switch room, at the end of the hall," she answered, her voice a little weak.

"Sarah, do you think you can get Rebecca out of here on your own?" I asked.

Rebecca crossed her arms. "I'm fine."

"I can do that." Sarah nodded, ignoring her sister's protests. "Let's go." She gently tugged Rebecca's arm.

I grasped Rebecca's hand for a moment. Her glare softened into a smile, and she turned to Sarah. "The stairs are in the first room. We should probably take those."

I watched the twins walk away until Matthew nudged my ribs. "Focus on the mission."

"Right." I saluted. "I'm entirely focused, like always."

"Says the man who gets distracted thinking about doughnuts every day," Daniel retorted.

"Well, I wasn't thinking about doughnuts, but now that you mention it—"

"Save it," Matthew cut in, obviously not feeling the same sense of relief Daniel and I felt. "Rebecca said MAX should be in the room at the end of the hall. What we want is video evidence, and the FBI will take care of everything else from there. All we need to do is plant a camera and get out."

"We don't happen to have a small, robotic camera we can drive under the door, do we?" I asked, already knowing the answer.

Matthew shook his head. "Since sneaking into the office didn't work, what should we do now?"

I thought for a minute. "Too bad I ditched my Jack wig. I could've gotten in as Jack and gotten video that way."

Daniel's eyes lit up. "I've got it."

These handcuffs are about as comfortable as sandpaper lotion, I thought, wishing they were slightly looser. My captors knocked on the door at the end of the hall. The door swung open, and I was shoved inside, once again face-to-face with MAX and five more guards.

"We found one of the intruders, sir," my shorter captor, aka Daniel, said. Daniel and Matthew had traded uniforms with some of the guards we'd knocked out. They handcuffed me, wired me with video and audio recording, and headed to the switch room.

MAX rolled his eyes. "You again?"

"Long time no see," I replied, a grin sneaking into my face. I glanced around the room. Shelves of electronics and power boards lined the room, and the center of the room held a giant metal box like the one Daniel and I found in Colorado—a computer on the left side, a bunch of switches, a big lever on the right, and blinking lights all over the face of the box.

"Jack found out who you are—Luke Mason from Truth Squad. You've saved him the time of tracking you down by coming back. Very thoughtful of you."

"I try to be."

MAX huffed. "I'll be frank with you—we cannot let you live. Not after all the time you've spent here. We both know that you know too much."

I raised an eyebrow. "Yet I'm still here." *And this is great footage.*

"Good point. You're leverage. Because we also know who you are to Rebecca."

I felt my face flush at those words. *Great.* "Why does that matter?"

"We lost our leverage with Isaac—thanks to you. But now we have new leverage because you returned to try to be the hero to your damsel in distress," MAX said, rolling his eyes in disgust. "I need Rebecca's codes today, and you're the reason she'll give them."

"I don't know—she's pretty stubborn," I replied. "You're probably not getting those codes. Besides, we both know you can go on without them."

"No!" MAX yelled, his hands balling up into fists. "I will not let Zaiden have the upper hand on this one."

"Hard to have the upper hand when you're in jail," I muttered. That comment got a slap in the face, and I quickly regretted it.

"All of my switches are stuck for twenty-four hours unless I have the code," MAX ranted, pacing around the room. "I should've expected Zaiden to do something like this to maintain control. So, it's time that stubborn brat told me the answers to Zaiden's codes."

I rolled my eyes. "I don't think that'll be happening any time soon."

"What do you mean?"

"That 'stubborn brat' left," I said, lifting my chin defiantly. Daniel gave me a look. *Probably shouldn't have said that.*

"She what?" MAX stared at me blankly. After an awkward five seconds, he pushed a button on his watch and an alarm sounded.

"LOCKDOWN MODE ACTIVATED," a robotic voice boomed through the speaker.

Definitely shouldn't have said anything, I thought. Daniel's tightened grip confirmed that he was thinking the same thing.

MAX turned to a guard beside him. "Go find Rebecca Sanders." The guard nodded and hurried from the room.

"Sir, where would you like us to take him?" Matthew asked, nodding his head toward me.

MAX shook his head. "Nowhere. I want him to stay here. He's my leverage for when Rebecca gets here." He turned his glare toward me. "And that leverage is more effective when she can see it."

I gulped. *Lord, we've got our video evidence now. So, please help the FBI to hurry it up.*

For the next five minutes, MAX messed around with the box of switches, trying to get more of them to turn, but nothing was working. He really did need Rebecca's codes. I was bored of watching MAX's frustration, so my brain drifted to Rebecca and Sarah, wondering whether they'd gotten out of the building fast enough before the lockdown. *Why do I always have to make silly mistakes like this? Someday I'll learn to think before I speak.* My mind drifted to doughnuts after the mission, and this time I'd be able to get a doughnut for Rebecca.

The door slammed open, bringing my mind back from apple fritters to see the twins roughly escorted into the room by two guards. My hopeful thinking that they'd made it out was quickly crushed.

"Oh, wonderful. Your double is here, too," MAX said, glancing between the sisters. Today they were easy to tell apart—Rebecca had bruises and looked exhausted, and Sarah's pale face wavered between fear and boldness.

Rebecca's training came to life and her exhausted face took on her typical sarcastic expression. "What does that matter to you?"

MAX grabbed her chin and turned her head to look first at Sarah, then me. "Do you see who's here? Their lives are in your hands now. You give me the codes, and until you do—because I know you will—you can watch them suffer."

I could see Matthew's eyes darting around. He was obviously trying to come up with a plan. There were now six guards in the room, MAX, and five Truth Squad agents. *The FBI have got to get here, soon,* I thought.

MAX snapped at a guard. "Get to work." The guard slid some short spikes over his fingers and flexed his fist.

Maybe Matthew will think up a plan sooner. I glanced at Matthew. He still seemed to be processing.

The guard took a swipe at my bicep. Blood dripped down my arm. I couldn't hide my grimace. "Hey, this isn't a fair fight," I said, glaring at MAX.

MAX glared at me. "That's because you're not a part of this fight. This is a fight between my will and hers." He turned to Rebecca. "What's the code for 'better watch your back; you never know who's after you'?"

Rebecca's mouth was clamped shut. The guard socked me in the stomach. Luckily my bulletproof vest kept the spikes from doing more than prick me. By the third punch to the gut, I was ready to puke.

"Fifteen," Rebecca exclaimed.

"Don't give the codes," I grunted, trying not to puke.

An alarm sounded. "Someone's gotten through the lockdown," a guard said.

"Go check the security cameras," MAX ordered the guard, who quickly left.

Moments later he ran back into the room. "It's the FBI!"

Praise the Lord! I sighed with relief.

"No, no, no—" MAX glanced frantically around the room, fear slowly entering his eyes. "Not after all this," he muttered. He shook his head. "Follow me," he called to his guards, "and bring the prisoners. They know too much."

"Why not just get rid of them now?" the guard with the spikes asked. "They'll just slow us down."

"We'll get rid of them in the tunnel. We can't let them be found."

"Sir," Matthew jumped in, blocking MAX's exit from the room. "Why not blame their deaths on Jack? This is your chance to cut ties with him."

MAX's wild expression calmed down. "You're right. Where is Jack?"

"Out cold in the room Rebecca escaped from, sir," Matthew replied.

"Take the prisoners there, execute them, and then meet me at the tunnel," he said to Matthew.

"Yes, sir," Matthew said, continuing to stand in the doorway.

MAX slapped Matthew. "Get going!"

Matthew nodded and stepped out of the way. Just then, a battering ram hit through the door. "FBI, everyone on the ground!" a voice yelled.

"Yes!" I exclaimed. Daniel helped me to the ground with my handcuffs. "I am so ready for a nap!" I looked across the room and smiled at Rebecca who also lay on the floor. *Me too,* she mouthed.

CHAPTER 14

"That's gonna leave a good scar," Daniel joked, sitting down next to me. A paramedic was wrapping up my bicep. Luckily, I didn't need stitches, just a few butterfly band-aids.

MAX was on his way to prison, and we now had access to all of his files. Mr. Truth and Agent Brandon were already working on sorting through everything to separate MAX's underground operation from his cover-up operation, JX Headquarters.

"I wonder if I can get a refund for my tux," I said. "I'm not sure I want to wear a JX designer suit for my wedding after all this."

Daniel laughed. "No kidding."

"Did the video recording transmit okay to Truth Squad?" I asked.

Daniel nodded. "They sent it out to the major news outlets thirty minutes ago. The story should already be out about the FBI raid here, though. I've already seen press trying to get statements from behind the yellow tape out front."

"Good." I thanked the paramedic for her help as she moved on, then closed my eyes for a moment. My adrenaline had calmed down, and my sleepless night was catching up with me. I knew the day was far from over—the FBI wanted statements from all of our team involved in this mission. Mr. Truth expected that we would stay in D.C. for another week or so to get things unraveled before heading home. *Thank You, Lord,* my tired brain managed the most heartfelt thank You possible.

"Have you heard from Sarah at all?" I asked, my eyes still closed.

Daniel laughed. "They left fifteen minutes ago. You'll need a little more patience than that."

"Whatever." The paramedics recommended that Rebecca go to the hospital to make sure she didn't have any internal bleeding from the beating she took. She wanted to refuse, but Mr. Truth required her to go. Plus, she needed the tracker removed from her arm properly, and she was probably dehydrated. Sarah went with her as moral support. I wanted to be moral support, but Mr. Truth also required me to stay on site for interviewing, since I had been the undercover agent this whole time.

Agent Brandon drove Daniel and me to FBI headquarters for giving our statements. The rest of the day was spent answering questions, signing papers, answering more questions, and signing more papers. We heard that FBI searched the top four floors of the JX headquarters and found files on all the powerplants MAX had infiltrated as well as copies of correspondences between MAX and others, including Zaiden.

It was late by the time we got back to our hotel, and Rebecca had long since gone to bed. Sarah informed us that the doctors said she was okay; she was given some fluids and had some stitches in her arm from removing the tracker. She mostly needed rest. So, I went to bed impatient for morning to come, and thanking God that Rebecca was finally safe.

The next morning, we all headed back to FBI headquarters, ready to give more statements and sign more papers. This time I rode in the car beside Rebecca, holding her hand and knowing she was safe.

"I'm never letting go of your hand, ever again." I grinned.

Rebecca smiled. "Never?" I shook my head. "Even to give me a hug?"

"Well," I shrugged, "that's the only exception."

She laughed. "Good!"

We spent the whole week answering questions and signing papers. I also learned that I couldn't get a refund on a tux from a company that was now under investigation.

"You already bought the ring, so you don't need to worry about the tux. Just enjoy owning it," Daniel said.

I glared at him. "Says the man who still has money in his bank account."

"True, true," Daniel said with a smirk. "But seriously, we've got some planning to do."

I nodded. "That we do."

"We're going hiking right now? In dresses?" Sarah asked as we walked out of church.

Rebecca laughed. "It's not a hike. It's a walk."

Sarah looked down at her feet. "Even if it's just a walk, I wore heels today."

Daniel smiled. "We won't be walking fast. We'll call it a stroll."

Sarah shrugged. "If you say so."

I grinned at Rebecca and double-raised my eyebrows. She smiled back. We both knew what was really going on. We'd been back from D.C. for three weeks. It had taken about that long for Truth Squad and the FBI to go through all of MAX's paperwork. It was insane how many names and places across the US were involved in this scheme. It was going to take a long time to fully unravel. MAX still hadn't even had his trial yet. But the public was finally aware that he was no longer a candidate for president, nor was he ever a good candidate to vote for. For a couple weeks, the public had tried to claim that Truth Squad had interfered with the election. But once the undercover video we'd taken had gone viral, the rumors about Truth Squad slowly calmed down. The election was able to happen peacefully, and a good man had been elected by the people.

Now, it was time for Daniel's plan to take effect. It took him three weeks to decide where he wanted to propose. Rebecca had said it needed to be somewhere beautiful, but not somewhere like the beach where Sarah would suspect something was up. Daniel finally settled on a small lake amidst some walking trails not too far from Truth Squad headquarters. And he decided to spring it on Sarah right after church as though it were a spur-of-the-moment thought. That way they would be dressed up.

Rebecca gave her stamp of approval to this plan. "She'll love it," she'd said.

Early that morning, Rebecca, Daniel, and I had gone to the lake and set up a picnic area with flowers and balloons. Matthew agreed to get there before us with a camera to hide and take pictures of the moment. Rebecca made sure we picked the perfect spot for pictures and made sure all the decorations were fitting for what her sister would love. Her attention to detail over everything that would make this day perfect for Sarah made me smile. I hoped it would be perfect for Rebecca, too.

We drove to the walking paths and parked near a short trail up to the lake. "The weather is perfect for walking today," I said, giving Rebecca my hand as she stepped out of the car. The air was crisp and energizing when you inhaled, but it was still sunny.

Rebecca and I followed behind Daniel and Sarah. We had to walk slowly up the graveled path since Sarah wore heels, but I didn't mind. I enjoyed seeing Daniel and Rebecca's nervousness. They both wanted this moment to be perfect.

Finally, we made it to the top of the hill to see the lake. The smooth water perfectly mirrored the evergreen trees surrounding it and the blue sky above, almost like you should be able to step into the water and find yourself among upside down trees. It was quiet, with just the chirping birds and chattering squirrels scurrying through the trees for a soundtrack.

We walked around the lake, then came upon our picnic setup, a red and white checkered blanket surrounded by red balloons tied to the trees. On the blanket sat a picnic basket and several vases of red carnations.

Sarah gasped. "What's this?"

"A picnic," Daniel replied, smiling at her.

"So, this is why you insisted we go on a walk?" Sarah clasped her hands excitedly. "It's beautiful! Look at the flowers!"

"I'm glad you like it," Daniel said, nervously fidgeting with his hands. I had to bite my lip to hold back my laughter. "But this isn't the only reason I wanted to come here."

Sarah looked confused. "What do you mean?"

Daniel got down on one knee and pulled a box from his pocket. "Sarah, I've loved getting to know you better these past couple years, and I want to spend the rest of my life with you." He opened the box, to reveal the ring he'd so carefully picked out, a heart-shaped diamond with blue jewels on each side. "Sarah Sanders, will you marry me?"

Her hands flew to her mouth and her jaw dropped. "Are you serious?"

Daniel smiled. "Of course I'm serious."

Sarah's eyes watered as she nodded. Daniel carefully slid the ring on her left ring finger, then gave her a hug.

I glanced at Rebecca. She was smiling from ear to ear. "Beautiful moment," I murmured, my heartrate picking up. *This is it.* I slowly stepped back from Daniel and Sarah.

Rebecca nodded, following me a short distance away from the happy couple. "This is exactly what she was hoping for—to be surprised." She smiled at me. "It's perfect."

I grinned back. "Almost perfect. There's just one thing that could make it more perfect."

"Oh, really?" Rebecca raised an eyebrow, a playful smile spreading across her face.

I nodded. "For sure." I started walking again toward a spot by the water a few paces away with a clearing from the brush to see the lake. "Rebecca, there's so much I want to say. I'm so thankful for you, and this whole adventure we've been on the past few months has made me ten thousand times even more thankful for you." I stopped walking and turned to face her. Seeing the huge smile on her face made the rest of the speech I had prepared vanish. "Well, I forgot what else I was going to say, so," I put a shaking hand into my pocket and pulled out a small box. I got down on one knee and opened the box. "Will you marry me?"

She laughed. "Of course!"

"Yes!" I jumped up and spun Rebecca around, then pulled her into a hug.

She pulled back, laughing. "Um, you forgot something." She held up her left hand and wiggled her fingers.

"Oh, yeah!" I laughed and grabbed the diamond ring from the box, sliding it onto her finger.

Sarah and Daniel walked over and joined us just then. "Wait—are we twinning again?" Sarah asked, laughing as the two sisters showed each other their rings. Daniel and I fist-bumped.

Rebecca smiled at Sarah, then at me. "Would we really do anything else?"

THE END.

Printed in the United States
by Baker & Taylor Publisher Services